A Profe[illegible] Fighting Machine...

He thundered toward me, one step at a time. I began backing up. The brute had crossed over the line into Dangerous Territory, and my mind was racing.

"Steel, I must warn you that I'm an expert in Dog Karate."

He stopped. "Nah you ain't."

"Yes, I am."

"Ain't."

"Am."

"Yeah, but I'm twice as bigger than you, and three times as meaner."

"With karate, it doesn't matter."

He glanced over at Scamper. She was sitting up now, watching the show with sparkling eyes. "Hey Scamp, he says he knows fightin' tricks."

"Well, he's pretty tricky."

"So...what do you think?"

She fluttered her eyelashes. "All I can say is, I'd just *hate* to be the cause of a big fight."

He turned back to me, and a deep growl rumbled in his throat. "You're toast!"

Are you sure you want to hear this?

the Troublesome Lady

John R. Erickson

Illustrations by Gerald L. Holmes

Maverick Books, Inc.

MAVERICK BOOKS, INC.
Published by Maverick Books, Inc.
P.O. Box 549, Perryton, TX 79070
Phone: 806.435.7611
www.hankthecowdog.com

First published in the United States of America by Maverick Books, Inc. 2017.

1 3 5 7 9 10 8 6 4 2

Library of Congress Control Number: 2017909241

978-1-59188-170-4 (paperback); 978-1-59188-270-1 (hardcover)

Printed in the United States of America

Dedicated to the memory of ReAnna Wilson,
our granddaughter, who left us much too
soon in 2017. We think of her every day,
especially when we sing "Silly Old Maid."

CONTENTS

Creeped Out By Creepy Sounds

It's me again, Hank the Cowdog. It must have been the middle of the night, yes, a very dark night, and I was awakened by creepy sounds.

I lifted my head and glanced around. That proved pointless because...well, when it's dark, you can't see anything, right? But the hairs along my backbone knew something was wrong. They were switched into the Automatic Circuit, don't you see, and had raised themselves.

In my line of work, we pay attention to those hairs. That might sound ridiculous, a Head of Ranch Security taking notice of a bunch of hairs. I mean, a hair doesn't have eyes or ears and can't even bark, so what could a hair know that I don't know better?

Great question. I don't know the answer. All I can tell you is that time and experience had taught me to respect those hairs that grew along my backbone, and in the middle of that dark night, they were telling me to wake up and pay attention.

So...there I was, and let me be honest, I didn't have the faintest idea *where* that might have been. Zero idea. All I knew was that wherever I was, it was darker than the inside of a black cow at midnight, so I lifted Earoscanners and did a rapid scan.

Data Control chewed on that for a few seconds, then flashed a report: "CREEPY SOUNDS!"

I reached for the microphone of my mind. "Unit One to Drover, over. Stand by for an APB, repeat, APB. We're picking up creepy sounds, repeat, creepy sounds. Report in at once, over."

I cocked my ear and listened. I heard a faint voice. It said (this is a direct quote) it said, "Pork chop skiffer muttering miracles."

"Drover, is that you, over?"

"Over the clover, under the thunder."

"Drover, identify. Repeat, identify. Give me the secret password, over."

"Toad stools forever."

"That checks out, so you're Drover? Good. Do

you have any idea where we are?"

"Howdy cloudy puddin' and pie, kissed the girls and made 'em cry."

"Drover, please pay attention. This could be very important. Where are we?"

There was a moment of silence...well, not exactly silence. I heard grunting and snorting, then a voice: "Hank? Is that you?"

"Affirmative."

"Where are we?"

"I just asked you that."

"I'll be derned. What did I say?"

"You said, 'Where are we?'"

"Gosh, maybe we don't know where we are."

"Roger that."

I heard him yawn, then, "Gosh, it's dark. How come you woke me up?"

"I woke you up because...I don't remember. Do you remember?"

"Well, let me think. You said something about a big hairy ape."

"Not an ape. It was APB. I sent out an urgent All Points Burger."

"Boy, I love burgers."

"An All Points *Bulletin*."

"But I can't handle the onions."

"Please stop talking about burgers and

concentrate. Do you have any idea where we are or what we're talking about?"

"Not really. All I know is you woke me up."

"Okay, that gives us a starting point. You were asleep."

"Yeah, and I bet you were too."

"Exactly. We were both asleep. The question is, where?" At that point, I became aware of a moaning sound. "Wait. Listen. It's coming back to me. I heard a creepy sound. Do you hear that?"

"Oh my gosh, yes! Help, murder, let's hide!"

"Hold your position, soldier. We can't hide until we figure out where we are."

"Oh rats. Should we bark?"

"I'd better check Data Control." I sent an urgent message to DC and got clearance. "Okay, we've been cleared for barking. Load up Number Three Warning Barks and don't hold anything back. Ready? Fire!"

Boy, you should have heard us. Even though we couldn't see the target, we started pumping out the barks, big ones, the kind that throw a dog backward on every blast. I mean, the recoil on those Number Threes is pretty amazing. A lot of dogs can't handle it, but on this outfit, we do it all the time.

Well, we had been creeped out by creepy sounds, caused by unknown forces we couldn't see, but then a light came on in the distance.

Drover noticed and stopped barking. "Gosh, did we do that?"

"Of course we did, nice work." I glanced around and things began coming into crocus. Into focus, let us say. "All right, men, listen up. We have identified our location. We're in Slim's house, in the living room."

"Yeah, but what were those creepy sounds?"

"We don't know yet, so we'd better keep up the cover fire. Let's crank 'em out!"

Knowing that we were in Slim's house gave us a sense of confidence, and we were able to put heart and soil into our barking effort. Boy, did we bark! But then...was that a voice? Yes, a voice came booming down the hallway from the room from which the light was whiching, and it said, "Hank, dry up!"

Huh?

Dry up? How could we dry up and bark at the same time? Wait, hold everything. Have you noticed the clues here? There were several but you'll never see them unless you pay attention, so pay attention. Check this out.

Early Morning Clue List

- Maybe the voice belonged to Slim Chance.
- He often spoke to us in that rude manner.
- If the voice was Slim's, then so was the house, because Slim lived in his own house. To express that with Higher Math, we can write a formula: Slim's house + Slim's voice = Slim.
- Wow, is that cool or what? But there's more.
- Drover and I had spent the night on the floor in Slim's living room.

- I had been awakened from a peaceful sleep by certain creepy sounds.
- Even though we had figured out our location and the source of the voice down the hall, we still hadn't identified the source of those creepy sounds.
- Drover and I should have continued our Barking Procedure (#3 Warning Barks), but Slim had trashed that idea by yelling, "Dry up!"
- "Dry up" means "Quit barking."
- Hencely, we had to shut down the operation.
- But at least we knew where we were: Slim's shack.

End of Early Morning Clue List

Can you name another dog in Texas that could come up with a Morning Clue List like that, and I mean whip it out on the spot? Don't even bother to think about it, because I can tell you. There wasn't another dog in Texas, not even a dog in Oklahoma, who could have punched out such an awesome list of clues.

There's a word for that: WOW!

So, yes, Drover and I had spent the night at Slim's place and we'd barked him out of bed and here he came down the hallway, moving like a man under water. And let me tell you, he looked...how can I say this?

He looked *awful*: red slanty eyes, hair going every-which-way, wrinkled face that still held the impressions of his pillow, and thin pinched lips that looked like something made out of cement. And he was wearing nothing but boxer shorts and a T-shirt.

There's a word that describes him: YIPES!

I mean, I knew the guy, I knew he wasn't a monster or a vampire, but still...well, he looked like a monster and a vampire, so what's a dog supposed to do? I barked at him, by George, because in the Security Business, we bark first and ask questions later. We take no chances.

Don't laugh and don't forget that misters are monsters of mastery...monsters are masters of mystery, there we go. They're liable to show up in chicken suits or disguised as the mailman, we never know, and don't forget that there's a spy working undercover on our ranch: the cat.

So, yes, I gave him a blast of barking (the monster, not the cat), just to be on the safe side, and if I had it all to do over again, I'd do it all over again, because in the Security Business, we can't take chances. I've already said that, but it bears repeating and I'm scared of bears. If you're not scared of bears, you've never met one.

Who brought up the subject of bears? I have no idea. Does anyone know what we were talking about?

Phooey.

This is frustrating.

Wait, the cat. Yes, Sally May's rotten, pampered little never-sweat of a cat. Pete. She thought he was perfect, but we had proof that he was working on the sly for the Charlies. No kidding.

When things go to pot around here, we always know the source: Pete. But we weren't talking about Pete.

Tell you what, let's take a little break, walk around, get some fresh air, clear our heads, and come back in five minutes. I'll study the Morning Clue List and we'll mush on with the story.

Five minutes and don't be late.

Roundup Morning

Okay, everyone take a seat and let's get on with this, and you might want to take some notes.

Before the break, we were having trouble remembering the purpose of this conversation, but we've got that worked out. Slim Chance, the hired hand on this ranch, was groping his way down the hallway at some weird hour of the night, a time when most people and dogs should have been asleep.

That brings us up to seed. Up to speed, let us say, and when I saw the guy, I barked at him because...well, because he looked almost exactly like our profiles of Charlie Monsters. He'd slept on his face and his hair looked like a hotel for rats, and any dog would have barked at him.

No, I take that back. Most ordinary dogs would have run and hidden, but I stood my ground and gave him a blast of barking. He said (this is a direct quote) he said, "Hank, if you don't shut your gob, I'm going to flush you down the pot."

Okay, it was Slim, no question about it, and you see how he is when he wakes up? Really grouchy, unbearable. Hey, I was just trying to do my job and he was threatening to flush me down the pot. Oh brother.

But I ride for the brand, I try to get along with these people, so I went to him, down-shifted the tail into Good Dog Wags, and tried to give him some comfort and support and, you know, tell him that the day might turn out okay.

"Get that nose away from me! I can't stand a cold nose in the morning."

Fine. If he didn't like my nose, I would use it to comfort someone else. What a grouch.

He dragged himself through the house, went to the front door, and threw it open, and that gave me the missing clue on the Morning Clue List. Remember those "creepy sounds" that had started this whole incident with the barking and so forth? Well, the creepy sounds had come from a strong norther that had blown in.

What's a norther? It's a cold front that packs strong winds that rattle the windows and moan through the eaves and cause the house to creak. We start getting those northers in the fall, and they're always creepy. This was October, so it was right on schedule.

He slammed the door and ran a hand through his rat's nest (hair) and stared at the floor. "Great. I've got to be ahorseback at daylight. Yesterday was a perfect day, but now we get a hat-chasing, dirt-eating, tail-freezing norther. Baloney."

Well, I could have told him about the norther and the cold wind. I'd picked it up on radar while he was snoring in his bed, but cowboys don't listen to their dogs. When we try to help, they tell us to dry up.

In many ways, this is a lousy job. Have I mentioned that before? Maybe so.

He shuffled back to his bedroom and started plundering through the closet for his Cold Weather Outfit. I wasn't there to watch, but I had a pretty good idea what he was looking for: silk long-john underwear, wool shirt, wool vest, brush jacket, silk wild rag, and lined gloves.

That was his Cold Weather Outfit. He hadn't worn it since last April and parts of it were scattered all over the house, just where he dropped them the last time he used them. If he'd asked my opinion, I would have suggested something sensible, such as, "If you'll put your stuff away in a certain place, you might be able to find it when you need it."

But he didn't ask my opinion and he had to chase down every scrap of clothing, and I had to listen to him mutter and grumble. You want to hear some of it?

"Where's my silks? The frazzling mice ate a hole in my vest! Somebody stole my wild rag. If the right glove's here, where's the left one?"

On and on. Oh, another thing I would have suggested, if he'd asked my opinion: "If you'll find your stuff the night before, you'll be ready to go in the morning." But he doesn't want any advice from his dogs.

It was kind of sad, really. I mean, what's the point of having a top-of-the-line, blue-ribbon cowdog on the staff...never mind. Don't get me started on this.

Whilst he was reinventing the world, I went looking for Drover. Had you noticed that he vanished when Slim came creeping out of the bedroom? He did, and we're talking about "poof."

I figured I'd find him hiding under the coffee table, one of his favorite bunker locations, but he wasn't there. I made a pass through the kitchen and found him hiding behind the trash receptacle.

"What are you doing back there?"

"Who was that guy?"

"It was Slim. This is his house. Who else would be coming out of his bedroom?"

"Well, he looked different. I didn't want to take any chances."

"Oh brother."

"Well, you barked at him."

"I did not."

"Did too."

"Did not."

"Too too too."

"Not not not!"

"Did too, and I took cover."

I heaved a sigh and searched for patience. "Okay, maybe I barked at him, but where were you when I needed backup?"

"I scrammed."

"Five Chicken Marks, and this will go into my report. Now come out of there. You look ridiculous."

"Oh, I think I'll stay here, just in case."

"Ten Chicken Marks."

I left him there, cringing behind the garbage container. What a weird little mutt. I've thought

many times about laying him off, but I can't bring myself to do it. It would break his mother's heart if he got fired. I mean, she always thought he'd grow up to be a bum and the sad part is that he did.

This gives you a little glimpse into the problems I face, running this ranch. The cowboys don't listen to their dogs and my assistant in the Security Division is a little scaredy-cat who hides behind trash cans. And cold northers blow in without consulting me.

Oh well, we trudge on.

A horn blew outside the house. An unidentified vehicle had arrived and Slim came thundering out of the bedroom. Good, he was wearing more than his underwear this time, and was actually dressed in his Winter Outfit.

I was just standing there, minding my own business, and he stampeded right over me. "Out of the way, dog, it's Loper, and I've still got to saddle my horse!"

Well, excuse me!

He blundered his way into the kitchen, opened the refrigerator, and grabbed his Portable Breakfast, a boiled turkey neck. Back in the living room, he took a bite, pulled on his brush jacket, slapped on his felt hat, grabbed his chaps and a flashlight, and yelled, "Dogs, *outside*, chop

chop! We're burning daylight."

For his information, we were *not* burning daylight. There wasn't any daylight to burn. It was still black dark, but I got his point. He wanted us out of the house. That must have been the hidden meaning behind "chop chop." It meant "hurry up." I guess. Who knows what these guys are trying to say?

While he took another bite off the turkey neck, he held the door open and I slipped outside. Drover lollygagged behind and squirted through the opening. Out on the porch, he felt the wind and said, "Oh my gosh, it's freezing out here!"

He happened to be right. That was a nasty, cold, north wind, and it cut like hot butter through a wooden nickel.

A pickup and stock trailer were parked in front of the house, the motor running and the lights on. Nobody had cleared this with me, so I rushed...okay, it was Loper, so I passed him through Security. I mean, he owned the ranch.

Slim switched on his flashlight and headed toward the saddle shed. Loper got out of the pickup and followed. "You're not saddled yet?"

"No, I ain't saddled yet, 'cause you showed up thirty minutes early. You said to be ready at seven. It's six-thirty. At seven o'clock, I'll be saddled and ready."

"Well, you're always thirty minutes late, so I came thirty minutes early."

"He told us to be there at daylight, seven-thirty. You can't gather cattle in the dark. What's the point of showing up early to a roundup?"

"I'd rather be early than late."

"I know. You think it's fun to show up early, so we can all stand around in the dark and talk about how dark it is."

Loper laughed. "Boy, you're a bundle of joy in the morning. You must have missed your coffee."

"I did, 'cause you pulled up in front of my house and started blowing your stinking horn—half an hour early."

"So no breakfast?"

"I'm eating it right now."

"Probably bacon and eggs, grits, hash browns, and pancakes with maple syrup."

"Turkey neck. You want a bite?"

"Ha. No. Hurry up."

They ducked their heads against the wind, held onto their hats, and headed for the saddle shed. I followed, just to make sure they didn't mess anything up. I have to keep a close eye on those two.

Slightly Naughty Behavior

Slim opened the saddle shed door, turned on the lights, and gave his horse a coffee can of oats. I knew the horse. They called him Snips and I didn't like him. In fact, I don't like horses in general. They all think they're hot stuff and some of them, like Snips, think it's fun to chase dogs and bite their tails.

I had a long history with this arrogant crowbait and knew that he showed no respect for the Head of Ranch Security. But don't get me started on that.

Whilst the big lug gobbled and slobbered his oats, Slim tried to saddle him, but that proved to be no ball of wax. You know why? The wind was screaming out of the north, and it kept blowing the saddle blanket off the horse.

On the third try, Slim turned to Loper. "Reckon you could lend a hand?"

"Back in the old days, cowboys saddled their own horses."

"Back in the old days, they stayed in the bunkhouse in weather like this."

"I hate to spoil the hired help." Loper picked up the blanket and held it on the horse's back, and Slim swung the saddle into place. The right stirrup hit Loper on the head. "Hey, watch what you're doing!"

"Well, get out of the way. This ain't the Powder Puff Ranch."

Those guys can go on like that for hours.

When Slim started pulling cinches, I took the opportunity to leave. I figured they could do the rest of the job without my supervision, and besides, I had some important business to take care of.

Maybe I shouldn't tell you, because, well, it involved some Slightly Naughty Behavior, and you know how I am about the kids. I try to be a good example, don't you see, and if I'm ever involved in SNB, I'd just as soon they didn't know about it.

I'm sure you understand. Sorry.

Drip
Coffee

Oh, maybe it wouldn't hurt, I mean, it wasn't *that* naughty. Tell you what, I'll let you in on the secret, but if it starts to seem Too Naughty, don't read any more. Just skip to the next chapter. Deal? Okay, here we go.

1. See, while Slim and Loper were yapping at each other, they revealed an important piece of information, and you might have missed it.
2. They were going to help a neighbor round up his cattle. (Our outfit swapped out cowboy work with the neighbors, don't you see).
3. I was pretty sure they wouldn't invite me to go with them on this adventure, because...well, they had some peculiar ideas about ranch work, such as, "When you go to help the neighbors gather cattle, leave the dogs at home."
4. That's hard to believe, isn't it? I agree, but I'm a loyal dog and most of the time I go along with their notions, even the weird ones. However...
5. We had seven or eight neighbors in this valley, including a guy named Billy and an old man named Woodrow.
6. Billy owned the most gorgeous collie-gal in

the entire state of Texas: the lovely, adorable, incomparably beautiful Miss Beulah.

7. Old man Woodrow had a daughter named Viola. She was engaged to Slim Chance, but she was crazy about ME.
8. Hencely, if they went to either of those ranches...heh, heh...I wanted to be there too, for obvious reasons.
9. Oh, be still my heart!

Do you get it now? If Loper and Slim thought I was going to miss out on an opportunity to see those ladies, they were crazier than bedbugs. Hencely, I wouldn't be staying home. It would involve me in some Slightly Naughty Behavior, but don't forget the Wise Old Saying:

Hm. I had it right on the tang of my tipper only a moment ago. Hang on a second.

I don't remember, skip it.

So there you are, a rare glimpse into the kind of long-range planning we have to do in my line of work. Pretty amazing, huh? You bet. Believe me, ordinary dogs never venture into these waters.

I trotted back to the house and found Mister Squeakbox sitting on the porch, out of the wind. "Okay, soldier, listen up." He rolled his eyes toward the dark sky. "Why are you rolling your eyes around?"

"Well, you said to listen *up*."

"Drover, you don't listen with your eyeballs. In fact, you hardly even listen with your ears."

"Sorry."

"Three more Chicken Marks, and stop rolling your eyes. I have some good news and some bad news."

"Can we skip the bad news? I hate bad news."

"Too bad. You need to toughen up. The good news is that I'm going to take our cowboy crew to a roundup this morning."

"In this wind?"

"That's correct. The bad news is that you can't go."

"Oh goodie!"

"I beg your pardon?"

"I said, oh rats."

"Don't argue with me. I've made my decision and it's final."

"So I'll have to stay here on the porch all day? Darn."

"I know you're disappointed, but it can't be helped. We need someone here to guard the house."

His eyes blanked out. "Against what?"

"Against anyone who might try to steal the porch or Slim's wood burning stove. If someone shows up..."

"I'll hide."

"You *won't* hide. You will stand your ground and blister them with a barrage of barking. Am I making myself clear?"

"Well, let me see." He pinched his eyes into a squint. "I'll stand in the garage...and bark their blisters?"

"Exactly, and if necessary, you'll go down fighting for your ranch." I gave the little mutt a pat on the shoulder. "Drover, I'm proud of you."

"That's weird."

"What?"

"I said, go team!"

"That's the spirit. Maybe we can take you on the next trip. Good luck, soldier, and be brave."

I whirled around and marched toward the pickup, before my emotions got the best of me. Hey, I'm pretty hard-boiled and mostly immune to emotional so-forths, but you have to admit that it was a pretty touching conversation. Very touching.

See, instead of whimpering and moaning, which would have been Typical Drover, the runt had stepped up to the challenge and accepted some responsibility. Those of us who are involved in training our men wait for such a moment, and I'll be honest, there had been times when I'd thought I wouldn't live long enough to see it in Drover.

That kind of discouragement comes with the job. We go through dark times when it seems that we're dealing with noodle-brains and meatheads, but then comes the day when we finally see a spark in their eyes and...well, it makes all our efforts seem worthwhile.

Sorry, I didn't mean to get carried away.

Anyway, I left my assistant guarding the house and marched straight to Loper's pickup, which was hooked up to a sixteen-foot gooseneck trailer. Loper's saddled horse had been standing inside the trailer. I didn't know which horse, maybe Sox or Happy or Deuce, but it didn't matter. You know my Position on Horses. I don't like 'em, never have. They are such braggers and bullies.

As I slipped past, he just *had* to flap his big fat mouth. "Oh great, a dog on roundup day, just what we need."

I ignored him. No, actually, I didn't. I stopped in my tracks and STUCK OUT MY TONGUE. There! That would teach him a lesson.

The big oaf mouthed off again, but I didn't hear it over the roar of the wind. Man alive, that wind was really getting after it. You know, very few dogs would have volunteered to go to work on such a day. You would find them huddled on the south side of the house, staring at swirling leaves and saying, "Duh-h-h-h." That's what your ordinary run of mutts say about everything: "Duh."

Oh well. I continued on with my mission. At the rear of the pickup, I did a quick Visual Sweep and saw Loper and Slim coming out of the saddle lot, Slim leading his crowbait of a horse.

I went into Deep Crouch, sprang upward with a mighty...BONK...ouch, hit my head on the neck of the gooseneck trailer, and tumbled back to the ground. Oof!

I heard rude snorts of laughter coming from the trailer (the horse), and I'm almost sure he said, "Oh, nice shot, doggie, nice shot!"

Fool. Moron.

As I've said before, a dog has to be very careful when leaping into the back of a pickup that's hooked up to a gooseneck trailer. That gooseneck hitch is made of heavy steel and it really...never mind.

I re-entered the launch data, went into Deep

Crouch, soared over the tailgate, missed the stupid gooseneck, and made a safe landing in the bed of the pickup. I could hear the cowboys coming, still arguing about nothing.

Would they find me and throw me out? To find out, you'll have to keep reading.

Coffee and Burritos

Okay, the north wind was roaring through the cottonwood trees and the cowboys were coming. I moved my freight to the front of the pickup bed, right behind the cab, and hunkered myself down into the Stealth Position. In SP, a dog becomes invisible to the naked eye and even to enemy radar.

Wait a second. Come to think of it, what is a "naked eye?" I'd never thought about that, but it sounds kind of peculiar. Do we have time to discuss this? Not really, I mean we've come to a tense moment in the story, but we need to take a closer look at this.

Number One: There's something special about the word "naked." Say it in front of a bunch of kids and see what happens. They'll start laughing. If you don't believe me, try it. I guarantee they'll laugh. Why? Because...I don't know. Ask a kid.

So that gives us our first pud of the peezle... the puzzle, that is, the first pid of the puddle... the first PIECE of the PUZZLE, there we go. When eyes run around naked all the time, the kids laugh about it.

Number Two: What would an eye be wearing if it wasn't running around naked? A dress? Blue jeans? Bib overalls? Cowboy boots? The truth is, *we just don't know*, because this discussion takes us to the very edge of scientific knowledge.

See, very little research has been devoted to this subject, and that's pretty strange, because, well, eyes have been around for a long time, hundreds of years, and everyone you meet has a couple of eyes, and we're talking about dogs, people, snakes, coons, and even cats with their sneaky yellow eyes.

Clearly, someone needs to tackle this subject and come up with some answers. How can the children of America concentrate on their schoolwork if they're always laughing about all the naked eyes in the classroom? It's a problem that needs fixing, and the sooner the quicker.

Now, let's see, where were we? Oh yes, it was

a cold morning in October and I had sneaked myself into the back of Loper's pickup, remember? You need to pay attention. Now we're truckin'.

Since I was scrunched down and hiding in the back of the pickup (in the Stealth Position, if you recall), I couldn't see them, but I could hear them as plain as day, even though the day was too dark to be plain. They opened the trailer gate, loaded Snips, and closed the trailer gate—exactly what I had figured they would do. In other words, my plan was working to perplexion.

But now we come to the scary part. They left the rear of the trailer and walked toward the cab of the pickup, which means they were walking right past the very spot where I was stealthing, and we're talking about inches away.

I took a gulp of air and...this is crazy. I couldn't believe it. What lousy timing! I grabbed a big gulp of air, don't you see, but it must have gone down the wrong pipe, and before I could take corrective measures, it came back up.

BORP!

The footsteps stopped and Slim said, "What was that?"

"I didn't hear anything."

"You burped."

"I didn't burp."

"Loper, there's no shame in burping in public, but a guy ought to have enough class to excuse himself."

"Will you hurry up? We're going to be late."

"Well, I'm just saying that you ain't running around with a bunch of heathens. On this ranch, we ought to have standards."

"Get in the pickup."

Their footsteps moved away. Whew! Boy, I had dodged a bullet there. How in the world that burp had whistled out, I couldn't imagine, but it demonstrates the importance of our Stealth Program. If I'd been in the Normal Position, I would have been discovered, captured, and pitched out of the pickup, and that would have done serious damage to the story. At this very moment, you'd be sitting in your room, crying, with no story to read.

Don't let anyone tell you that stealth technology isn't extremely valuable in Security Work, because it is. A lot of dogs don't use it because they don't know *how* to use it. On this outfit, we try to stay on the cuddling edge of technology, and that's the only reason we still have a story.

So there you are, a little glimpse into the secret workings of the Security Division.

The cowboys loaded up in the cab and off we

went, chugging down the county road. Only then did I dare sit up and look around. What I saw was…well, not much. It was still mostly dark, with a thin line of orange on the eastern horizon, so I shrank back into Stealth. My plan was still working.

Minutes passed, ten or fifteen or even twenty. We rumbled across a cattle guard and continued at a lower rate of speed. The pickup slowed and stopped. The motor shut off and the lights went out. Two doors opened and closed, and I heard some odd tinkling sounds. What in the world?

Okay, it was the sound of their spur rowels. Of course. They were both wearing spurs, don't you see, because they were fixing to spend several hours ahorseback. Maybe you missed that little clue. Not me.

Their footsteps seemed to be moving away from me, so I cancelled Stealth, raised up, and felt a blast of cold wind. Gag, it took my breath away. Even so, I was able to scope out the situation in the first light of dawn's first light, and suddenly realized…this wasn't Billy's place or Woodrow's either, which meant…

What a bummer. My love life had just been dealt a serious blow: no Beulah and no Viola. I had volunteered for this mission on a miserable windy day, and there would be no ladies to watch me in action!

Oh well, it was too late to spill the milk. It appeared that we had arrived at a set of corrals. Slim and Loper joined a group of figures gathered around a small propane stove in front of the saddle barn, out of the wind. The guy who owned the ranch stepped out and greeted them with a handshake, and Loper said, "Morning, Baxter."

Okay, Baxter was one of our rancher-neighbors. He had squinty eyes and a big mustache that covered his upper lip. He pointed toward the two-burner stove that was hooked up to a propane bottle. A big coffee pot sat on one burner and a cast iron skillet on the other. "There's scrambled eggs, bacon, and tortillas. Make yourself a burrito, and there's the coffee."

Slim went to the coffee pot like flies to a watermelon. We're talking about a man on a mission. Don't forget that he'd been honked out of bed and had missed his morning joe. He filled a tin cup and offered it to Loper, who seemed surprised and said, "Oh, thanks."

Slim smirked and said, "Pour your own. You ain't an invalid," and started slurping. Loper grumbled, shook his head, and built himself a burrito.

The stove burners threw off enough light so that I was able to recognize of the crew: Baxter and his wife, Cindy Lou; Lance and Frankie from Lipscomb; Dave Nicholson from the C-Bar-C; and Billy, from Wolf Creek. Loper and Slim made it a crew of eight.

They were all "neighbors," which meant they lived on ranches within twenty-five miles of Baxter's place. In the busy seasons (spring branding and fall weaning), they joined forces and "neighbored" to get the ranch work done. In other words, they worked together as a cowboy crew and helped each other.

They were dressed for a cold day and stayed close to the fire, chewing burritos, drinking coffee, and waiting for the sun to come up. I heard someone say, "Baxter, you sure picked a pretty day for this."

That drew a laugh and Baxter said, "Yes, and it's liable to get worse, but it's got to be done. We're going to gather the creek pasture. It's two square sections, thirteen hundred acres. Three riders go east with Cindy Lou, I'll go west with my three. When we get to the pens, we'll sort off the cows and throw the calves into the weaning pen, then put out hay and feed."

Everyone understood. They finished their

coffee, shut off the propane, and went for their horses. I wasn't quite ready to announce my presence, shall we say, and had reason to suspect that Loper and Slim wouldn't be thrilled to know that I had come along, so I ducked down and returned to the Stealth Position.

Above the whistle of the wind, I heard them open the trailer gate and unload their horses, who were so big and clumsy, their hooves made a lot of noise on the wooden trailer floor. Bam, bam, bam. When the trailer gate slammed shut, I peeked out and saw them swing up into their saddles and pull down their hats against the wind. They joined the others and rode off into the grayish-yellow light of dawn.

Well! I figured it would take them a couple of hours to gather the cattle. In the meantime, I had the whole ranch to myself, and plenty of time to check things out and get prepared to help them with the penning and sorting.

I dived out of the back of the pickup and went straight to the first item of business, checking the cast iron skillet to see if they had left some breakfast scraps. I hopped my front paws onto the....OW!

When you light a stove, it gets hot, right? That's how come you can make coffee and

scrambled eggs on a stove, but there's one thing you need to remember about stoves: the skillet stays hot for a while after the burners are shut off.

So I quit the skillet and began sniffing the ground near the stove, just in case the crew had dropped a few fragments of egg or bacon. That can happen when they eat burritos, don't you see. If they don't close the tortilla at the bottom, good things can fall out, and sure enough I sniffed out some fragments of egg and bacon, which I wolfed down with the passion of a wolf that hadn't eaten breakfast.

I was starving. Don't forget that I had started the day with a bachelor cowboy whose idea of breakfast was a cold turkey neck that looked like a dead rat, and he didn't share.

So, yes, I was pretty excited about finding... HUH? Did you hear that voice? Maybe not, because you weren't there, but I was almost sure that I'd heard a voice. I froze, looked around, and saw...

You won't believe this.

A Big Old Hairy Thang

Are you still with me? Good. This is going to knock your socks off.

Okay, I was down at Baxter's place, checking for scraps in front of the saddle house, right? And my mind was occupied with very important matters, such as locating bacon bits, fragments of scrambled egg, and stub-ends of flour tortillas on the ground.

Hey, this was my only opportunity to scrounge up a breakfast, so I was very intent on locating every artiful add-a-fact…every edible artifact that might have fallen from eight breakfast burritos, and I had to do it in a hateful north wind that was causing dust and hay fragments to swirl through the air.

It was no easy deal and I was giving it Maximum Concentration, but then a voice seemed to be dripping through the coffee filter of my mind. At first, I ignored it, I mean, the cowboy crew had left to gather cattle and I was supposed to be alone, but something about the voice caught my attention.

It said, and this is a direct quote, it said, *"Well, hello there, you big old hairy thang!"*

There was something familiar about that voice, and I was almost sure that I had heard those very words before, delivered in the same sultry tone of vone.

Slowly, I rotated my head to the direction from which the voice seemed to be coming, and saw....HOLY SMOKES! The voice belonged to a certain lady dog I had met before, the mysterious Miss Scamper, She Of The Sultry Voice, who on several occasions had addressed me as "You Big Old Hairy Thang."

Wow.

How many lady dogs would be bold enough to talk that way? I mean, it was true, I *was* a Big Old Hairy Thang, but I couldn't imagine Miss Beulah saying that, nor any of the hundreds of lady dogs I had encountered in my career, who had absolutely flipped over my...

Maybe we should go over the list. They had flipped over my proud nose, deep intelligent gaze, enormous shoulders, a very sensitive tail that could express a wide range of emotions, and ears that could have been in a fashion show; amazing athletic ability, leadership skills, gifts in poetry, floposophy, music, literature, ranch management, and crinimal justice, and on top of that: dashing, smashing, drop-dead good looks.

The point is that Miss Scamper had taken notice, and had managed to compress her admiration into one amazing sentence: "Hello there, you big old hairy thang!"

So, yes, this was one of those Wow Moments we dream about. I was so smitten by her sudden appearance, I gasped and my eyes bugged out. My mouth dropped open and a nice hunk of scrambled egg rolled off my tongue.

She seemed amused. "You, ah, dropped something."

"Yes ma'am, it might have been my teeth and eyeballs."

"That happens a lot. It makes me wonder... do you suppose...well, could it be ME?"

"Yes ma'am, I'm pretty sure it's you."

She fluffed at her ears. "Huh. I try not to be, ah, conspicuous."

"I guess that hasn't worked out so well."

"Really? I just don't understand it." She walked a circle around me, or maybe I should say she "strutted" a circle around me, because that's the way she moved, in a strut. "Haven't we, ah, met before?"

"Yes ma'am, several times."

"Don't tell me the name. You're…Joey, right?"

"Uh…no."

"Freddie?"

"No."

"Oh right. Jasper!"

"I'm Hank the Cowdog, ma'am, and I'm sure you remember me."

"Oh, sure. You live in town, right?"

"I'm Head of Security on a ranch west of here, huge outfit."

"Oh sure. So…you're a cop or something?"

"That's part of my job, yes ma'am. Maybe you'd like to hear about it."

"Maybe later." She saw the hunk of scrambled egg on the ground, and sniffed it. "I must have interrupted your, ah, breakfast."

"No problem, it was just a snack."

"So…you don't want it?"

"Well, to be honest, ha, you're more interesting than scrambled eggs."

She fluttered her long eyelashes. "I hardly know what to say. May I?"

"May you what?"

"Finish your snack? It would be a shame to, ah, waste it."

"You bet, help yourself."

She nibbled the egg and gave me a long, sultry look. "Well, ah, how come you've stayed gone so long? You never come around to see me."

My heart almost stopped. "I…I…I stay pretty busy with my work."

"Oh right, the job. You mentioned that."

"Actually, ma'am, it's more than a job. In the first place…" Her gaze drifted away and she took a deep breath, almost as though…well, almost as though her mind had wandered. "Hello, yoo-hoo? Miss Scamper?"

Her gaze returned. "You talk a lot, don't you?"

"Thanks, and let me point out that when the cowboys come in with the herd, I'll be putting on a demonstration of cowdog skills. You'll be amazed."

"Umm, I don't think so."

"I beg your pardon?"

"Cow work is so…" She wrinkled her nose. "…so slow. What else can you do?"

I didn't know what to say, but then it hit me. "Well, I'm a part-time musician. I write songs."

She stared at me. "Why?"

"Why? Well, to express complex emotions, I guess. Hey, I could do one."

"You know, I really..."

"A song written and sung just for you."

She took a slow, deep breath. "Oh swell."

She was really excited, so I belted out a very sweet and meaningful song, just for her. Here, check this out.

One-Room Heart

Miss Scamper, Miss Scamper, do I have
  a deal for you!
A one-room heart: front porch, big yard,
  extraordinary view.
It just came on the market, right about
  when you arrove.
It's heated in the winter with a nice wood-
  burning stove.

And I'll even furnish the fuel.
Heh. Letters from my old girlfriends.

Now I'll admit this heart of mine might
  show a bit of wear.
For years I tried to rent it out to a gal who
  really cared.
Miss Beulah the Collie had a chance. In

fact, she had a bunch.
But that's a deal I never closed. In fact, it ate my lunch.

She had another boyfriend, see.
A birddog, if you can believe that!

But never mind, that's in the past, what's done is done is done.
She had her chance. What can you say except that she was dumb?
She blew the opportunity, she really missed a treat.
My heart's back on the market at a price you just can't beat.

A little humor there, did you get it?
You can't *beat* the price. Heart *beat*. Ha ha. Awesome.

Miss Scamper, Miss Scamper, let's try to make a deal.
This one-room heart's available, the price is just a steal.
What do you think, my sugar plum, and can we make this work?
To answer yes, just wink one eye and I will go berserk.

It's the best little heart I've ever owned.

> And don't forget: I'm a big old hairy thang.
> You said so yourself.

I finished my song and took a bow. "What do you think?"

She seemed...well, distracted. "Actually, I'm not much into music. Do you, ah, do tricks?"

"I'm not sure what you mean."

"Tricks."

"You mean...yes, of course. Beneath the surface, ha ha, I'm a pretty tricky fellow."

That brought a smile to her lips. "Are you really? How fun! Let's, ah, see what you can do."

To be honest, I wasn't sure where this was going, but by George, if she wanted tricks, I would show her tricks. Anything for the ladies, I always say.

"Okay, Miss Scamper, we'll start off with our basic Begging Stance. Watch this." I sat down, lifted my front feet off the ground, balanced myself in the Sitting Position, and even moved my paws in the air. "What do you think?"

She gave me a frozen smile.

"Of course that's just a warm-up. Now we move into the next phase. Check this out." Before her very eyes, I moved upward from Begging, stood on my back legs, and get this, walked five steps!

"What do you think now, huh? Is this an awesome trick or what?"

She gave me a shrug of the eyes. "I've seen it before."

"Oh, I get it, you're pushing for the really good stuff."

"Yes, let's, ah, look at that."

"Okay, here we go. You'll love this."

Actually, I hadn't prepared for this and wasn't sure what kind of really good stuff I might come up with, but the audience was waiting and I had to think of something.

Then it came to me: the Front Leg Walk. It was in the Advanced Category. "Here we go, Miss Scamper, this will blow you away."

I grabbed a big gulp of air and loosened up the enormous muscles in my shoulders (I would need them). For five seconds, I turned my thoughts into a laser bean and concentrated on this rare and extremely difficult feat of physical so-forth.

I was ready. I pushed my back legs with such force that my hiney moved upward and my entire body rose to a vertical position, with all my weight resting upon my two front...

CRUNCH!

This was embarrassing. I've already said that

CRUNCH!!

it was a tough trick and maybe I shouldn't have tried it, but I did and...

Okay, the bottom line is that I went vertical, but the front legs more or less turned to mush, and I more or less crashed into the ground, nose-first. Did it hurt? You bet, but it hurt even worse when I heard chirps of laughter coming from the lady.

She giggled, "That was kee-ute!"

"I didn't think it was so kee-ute. It almost broke my nose off."

Her smile faded. "So, ah, that wasn't part of the act?"

I collected myself off of the ground and brushed the dirt off my nose. "Not exactly, but no dog has ever attempted that trick in a high wind. We're just lucky nobody was injured."

"Well, shucks." Her gaze drifted again. "Is that all the show?"

This woman was a tough case and I needed to close with a strong finish. I glanced around and saw...yes! A metal bowl sitting in front of the saddle house, a perfect prop for my last trick.

I had never done this one myself and had seen performed only once, by a blue heeler named Dixie. Could I rise to the occasion and pull it off?

To find out, you'll have to keep reading.

The Food Bowl Parade

I marched over to the bowl. "Okay, Miss Scamper, this next one is really special, so you'll need to..."

The saddle house had several windows on the south side, and she was looking at her face in the glass: primping, fluffing at her ears, smiling at herself, and fluttering her long eyelashes.

"Uh, Miss Scamper, the show is over here. Miss Scamper?"

At last her gaze swung around. "Oh, ah, were you waiting for me?"

"Yes ma'am, I have one last trick and it's awesome."

She turned back to the window glass for one last look. "Ooo! Well, let's see what you've got."

I began my prep—several deep breaths and several moments of deep concentration. The deep concentration was especially important on this one, and you'll understand why in just a second. I mean, this was a real killer of a trick.

We had a technical name for it, "Food Bowl Parade," and here's the basic concept. See, a dog uses his nose to push an empty food bowl around and around, and when it's done right, he's moving in a run, while keeping the bowl out in front of his nose.

If you think that's easy, try it yourself. It's incredibly difficult.

Plastic bowls will work for this presentation, but we prefer metallic bowls because, well, they make a lot of noise. They clank, and if you go to the trouble of performing the trick, you want all the sound effects you can get. A clanking bowl creates a certain atmosphere of drama, don't you see, and draws the attention of the...maybe this is obvious, so let's get on with it.

Okay, I went into my Opening Stance—all four legs spread, nose aimed straight at the bowl—and counted down to Launch, sprang into action and nosed the bowl around a big circle in front of the saddle house. Maybe you've seen hockey players moving the muck down the ice with effortless sweeps of the stick? Same deal here, effortless poetry in motion, but with a lot of great clanking sound effects and even some barks.

Hey, I had her attention on this one, but I wasn't done yet. For the grand finagle, I slipped my nose under the rim of the bowl, flipped it into the air, and actually CAUGHT IT WITH MY TEETH!

Incredible!

I set it on the ground in front of her and took a bow. "What do you say now, Miss Scamper? Was that cool or what?"

I could see that she was impressed. "I like your style, Wolfie. Maybe you should, ah, stick around for a while." Her eyelashes fluttered like butterfly wings.

I forgot to breathe. "Well, ha ha, we...we might be able to arrange that."

"Oh swell!" She fluffed at one ear. "But Steel won't like it."

"Who?"

She pointed to some big black letters on the side of the bowl: **STEEL**. "That was his bowl you were, ah, pushing around."

"Well, thank him for me. It's a dandy bowl. Who is he, your brother?"

"My boyfriend."

I stared at her. "Your *boyfriend*! You have a boyfriend?"

"Oh sure, always...but, ah, not always the same one." She winked.

"I had no idea..."

"A girl has secrets."

"Right, but still..." I began pacing, as I often do when I'm pursuing the Elusive Rabbit of Truth. "So who is this guy? Tell me about him."

"Well, I doubt that he could, ah, push a bowl around with his nose."

"That was really something, wasn't it? And you know what? I had never rehearsed that trick."

"I think I'm amazed." Her gaze wandered. "Steel's all right but, ah, kind of dull."

"Oh, good. Heh. That's a word nobody ever used to describe me."

"I'll bet not. But he gets, ah, jealous."

I stopped pacing. "Jealous? Your boyfriend gets jealous?"

It seemed an odd time for her face to light up in a smile. "Uh huh. He gets a little crazy...over me, I guess."

"Your boyfriend gets crazy jealous when you talk to other dogs, is that what you're saying?"

She nodded. "How crazy are we talking about?"

"Well, ah, he's always beating up my friends."

"He beats up...maybe you should have mentioned this sooner."

"I guess it slipped my mind."

I paced back to her. "Let's skip to the bottom line. Do you think I could whip him?"

She nuzzled me with her nose and whispered, "I don't know, big boy. Why don't you ask him?"

"Uh...no thanks."

"He's standing right over there."

"What!" I turned my head and saw... "Good grief! That's him?"

Her eyes were dancing and she nodded.

Well, my eyes weren't dancing. They had just bugged out of my head. The guy was...

You know what? We'd better skip the rest of this. As I've said before, *the little children don't need to know everything about my work*. Some of it is just too scary, no kidding, and some of it...

How can I say this? Some of it I'm not especially proud of, and the kids will get along just fine without knowing. In fact, they'll be a lot happier in the long run, honest, so let's just skip this part.

It's no big deal, it doesn't mean we're being chicken, and I have a plan, check this out. We'll start another chapter. We'll call it "Chapter 6.5: Scary Part Deleted." We'll skip to a more pleasant topic and choose it ourselves.

What do you think? No? You want to continue the original story, the one with Miss Scamper's boyfriend? Oh brother. Well, I tried to warn you and that's all a dog can do. Let's get it over with.

Okay, Miss Scamper had just tipped me off that she had a boyfriend, and worse, that he got crazy jealous when she talked to other dogs—a great time for her to tell me, right? I mean, he'd been standing right behind us when she nuzzled me with her nose and called me "Wolfie."

I turned and looked and...yipes! This is the part I didn't want you to hear, because he was HUGE and UGLY. He had big feet, thick chest and shoulders, a head like a catfish, long teeth, and eyes that seemed to glow like...I don't know what, maybe red hot coals in a fire of mesquite wood.

In other words, there was nothing in his face that made me wish to get better acquainted, and then he spoke in a deep, raspy voice that chilled my liver. He said, "Who's the dude, Scamp?"

She was radiant, which seemed a little strange. "Well, ah, his name is..." She turned to me. "Tell me your name again, sweetie."

I flinched. "Please don't call me that!"

"I'm terrible with names."

"Hank the Cowdog."

She turned back to the gorilla. "He's Frank the Plowdog and we're pretty good friends. I guess y'all haven't met."

Steel gave me a flat, ugly glare. "What's a plowdog? Never heard of it."

I tried to hide the quiver in my voice. "Actually, it's Hank the Cowdog. I head up the Security Division on a ranch west of here."

"So what?"

"I'm here to help with the cattle work, and I hardly know this woman."

Scamper fluffed at her left ear. "That's right, Steely. I wouldn't want you to, ah, get the wrong idea."

"Yeah, I'll bet." He stomped over to me and pointed a paw at the bowl. "You see the name on that bowl?"

"Uh...yes sir."

"That's my name. That's my bowl. Nobody comes on my ranch and pushes my bowl around in front of my girlfriend."

"She wanted to see some tricks."

"Yeah, this ain't the first time. Well, buddy, I'm fixing to show *you* some tricks." He began

pawing up dirt with all four feet.

Miss Scamper was all aflutter and stepped in between us. "Now boys, boys, be nice. I'd just perish if y'all got into a big fight...over me!"

"Out of the way, Scamp, this jerk is outa here."

She strutted out of the line of fire, and I heard her say, "I hardly know who to root for!"

Well, I had walked into a real mess here. Are you sure you want to continue?

A Professional Fighting Machine

Okay, I was in a real mess. Steel was all stoked up to do some damage on me and... wait a second. There was something fishy about this deal. Maybe you hadn't noticed and maybe I hadn't either, but I noticed it now.

I turned to the ape, who was shoveling up dirt with all four paws. "Listen, pal, before you get yourself all worked up, we need to talk."

He was grinding his teeth. "Nah, talk's over, man. We're on a train to Fight City."

"Just listen for two minutes."

He stopped shoveling dirt. "Okay, two minutes."

I moved toward him and lowered my voice. "Has it ever occurred to you that Scamper might be trying to stir up trouble?"

"She's *Miss* Scamper to you, jerk. Show some respect for the lady."

"All right, sorry. Miss Scamper. Had you thought that she might be trying to stir up trouble?"

"Nah, she wouldn't do that."

"No? What got you so stirred up?"

His eyes blanked out for a second. "Don't be talking about my girlfriend, it makes me crazy."

"Steel, I'm just citing facts. Look at her."

She was sitting off to the side, admiring the toenails on her left front paw. She must have noticed the silence and gave us a crabby look. "Well, are y'all going to fight or not? I've got things to do."

I turned back to him. "You see what I mean? She's trying to start a fight between you and me, and we've got nothing to fight about."

"Sure we do."

"What?"

"I don't like your face."

"Well, I'm not crazy about yours either."

"Don't be talking about my face, dude."

"Okay, you have a nice face."

"Now you're telling lies."

"What would you like for me to say about your face?"

He seemed confused. "I want you to shut your

face about my face, and I still hate your face, oh yeah."

"Fine, you hate my face, but that's no reason to get into a fight."

"So...what are you saying, man, that I'm some kind of stupid dog, huh? Is that what you're saying? 'Cause if that's what you're saying, that makes me even crazier, 'cause nobody calls me stupid and lives to call me stupid."

I took a deep breath and searched for patience. I mean, this was so silly! "Steel, nobody said you were stupid, and the whole point is that we have nothing to fight about."

He began walking a circle around me, and he was looking pretty crazy. "Oh yeah we do, oh yeah. You was messing around with my food bowl, and nobody messes with my food bowl."

"Steel, I merely used it as a prop for a trick."

"That's the whole point, jerk. Nobody but me props up tricks on this ranch, nobody."

"Yes, but you can't do this trick."

He stopped and glared at me with burning eyes. "What are you saying, frog face? That I can't do a trick with my own food bowl, on my own ranch? Huh?"

"Let's see if you can do it."

"Oh, you're really shopping for a hospital

now." He gave me a hard shove. "Out of the way."

He lowered his nose and advanced toward the bowl, and that's when it turned into comedy. See, he stepped on the rim with one of his clodhopper feet, and the bowl flew up and whacked him on the nose.

Bam!

He was shocked, but what did he expect? When you step on the rim of an empty bowl, it will fly up and whap you on the nose. It was so funny, I snorted a laugh.

Bad idea. His eyes became explosions of gasoline. "Oh, you've done it now, man, I can't stand to be laughed at, no way!"

"I'm sorry, it slipped out."

"Yeah, well, you're fixing to slip out too."

He thundered toward me, one step at a time. I began backing up. The brute had crossed over the line into Dangerous Territory, and my mind was racing.

"Steel, I must warn you that I'm an expert in Dog Karate."

He stopped. "Nah you ain't."

"Yes, I am."

"Ain't."

"Am."

BAM!!!
STEEL

"Yeah, but I'm twice as bigger than you, and three times as meaner."

"With karate, it doesn't matter."

He glanced over at Scamper. She was sitting up now, watching the show with sparkling eyes. "Hey Scamp, he says he knows fightin' tricks."

"Well, he's pretty tricky."

"So...what do you think?"

She fluttered her eyelashes. "All I can say is, I'd just *hate* to be the cause of a big fight."

He turned back to me, and a deep growl rumbled in his throat. "You're toast!"

Are you sure you want to hear this?

Okay, let's get it over with. The big ox jumped into the middle of me, buried me, and proceeded to hammer on me with all of his paws. Then he did a number on my ears with his teeth. I got the impression that this wasn't his first brawl.

Above the roar of Big Boy's growling, I could hear Miss Scamper chirping on the sidelines. "Ooo, good move! Now, you boys don't hurt anyone!"

I was getting creamed. Lucky for me, after using me for a mop for about five minutes, he ran out of breath and had to stop for air. I was able to scramble out of the grisp of his grasp, and burned a path straight to the pickup, went flying over the tailgate, and made a graceful landing in the back.

Whew! I knew I was safe back there, I mean, there was no way the big ape could jump that high, so I seized the opportunity to...well, mouth off and win back a few points. Hee hee. I love doing that.

I leaned over the side of the pickup and gave him a good blistering. "Steel, you're such a loser. You had me down and couldn't finish the job. Ha! You ran out of breath, for crying out loud! You're out of shape, pal. Real fighters stay in shape."

Now get this. A look of sadness swept over his face and he hung his head. Miss Scamper was watching, and she marched over to him. "I wouldn't let him talk to me like that!"

"Yeah, but he's right. I ain't worked out in three months."

Her gaze snapped back and forth between us. "Well, I never...is that all you can say?" He nodded his big head. She stamped her foot. "Steel, this is shameful! He was messing with your food bowl!" He nodded. "Now you jump yourself into that pickup, you hear? I've got a lot of stuff to do and can't be hanging around all day."

He wiped his nose on a paw and lifted his

head. “Okay, Scamp, I’ll do my best.”

“Well, you’d better!” She shot a glare at me and marched back to the sidelines.

His eyes swung up to me and gave me the shivers. “Okay, you little jerk, you’ve really, really done it this time. Here’s what happens to little jerks that mess with my food bowl.”

He backhoed some dirt with his paws and came tramping toward the pickup, like some kind of gigantic robot monster. “Steel, we need to talk.” He kept coming. “Okay, I apologize for the food bowl.” He kept coming. “Look, maybe I could pay rent on the bowl. What do you think?”

He was picking up speed and heading straight for the tailgate. His eyes were burning and he had a real bad snarl on his mouth. When he reached the pickup, he lunged upward, locked his front paws over the top of the tailgate, pulled, scrambled…and fell back to the ground.

My confidence came rushing back. “See, what did I tell you? That’s what happens when you keep your face in the food bowl all the time.”

Maybe I should have kept my mouth shut. Sometimes that’s a problem with me, I talk when I should…anyway, my words seemed to have, well, had an explosive effect on the big lug, and that was bad news.

He leaped to his feet and rolled the bulging muscles in his shoulders...and as I watched, I finally figured out what breed of dog he was: PIT BULL. Gag! I should have noticed before: the stocky build, the big ugly head, the yellow catfish eyes, the long teeth.

Gulp.

Pit bulls are notorious for their fighting skills, right? Oh brother, when will I ever learn? I had just mouthed off to an angry, jealous, insane, pit bull fighting-machine, and he was fixing to make a snack out of me.

Okay, you're the one who wanted to continue with the story. What should we do now?

A Secret Escape Route

So there we were: me in the back of the pickup, Steel rumbling and roaring about all the awful things he was fixing to do to my body, and Miss Scamper on the sidelines, flapping her long eyelashes and gasping in excitement.

But wait! What if this was just a bad dream and I was actually asleep on my gunny sack bed? Those things happen. I would wake up and see little Drover beside me, and we would laugh and share and laugh some more.

I waited to wake up. No luck there.

I glanced off to the east. Maybe the cowboy crew would suddenly appear, see that I was in big trouble, ride to my rescue, and put the monster on a leash. I would settle for that.

No luck there either.

I had one last card to play. "Steel, before we do anything we might regret, let's pause a moment and talk about the Brotherhood of All Dogs."

He stopped shoveling dirt and stared at me. "What's that supposed to mean?"

"It means that, beneath the skin and hair of our outward selves, we're both dogs."

"Yeah? So what?"

"Well, you and I have more in common with each other than with a tree."

He gave that some thought. "Huh. Never thought of that."

"See, we're united by our Dogness."

He nodded. "Yeah, but I don't want to whip a tree. I want to whip you."

"I know, but maybe we could have a cooling-down period and, you know, give it some more thought."

He shot a glance at his girlfriend. She gave her head three shakes. An eerie light appeared in his eyes. "Nah, I need to get this done before Baxter gets back. He don't approve of my methods." He cut loose with a laugh that froze my gizzard. "Har, har, har!"

Well, if he managed to climb over the tailgate,

I was cooked.

He shoveled some more dirt, backed off to get a good run at the pickup, rolled his beefy shoulders, winked at Miss Scamper...and here he came, like a freight train down the tracks!

He soared into the air, crashed against the tailgate, hooked his paws over the top, pulled and tugged and grunted...would he make it over the top? He pulled and tugged and grunted...and CLIMBED INTO THE BED OF THE PICKUP!

Well, I would soon become the Late Head of Ranch Security. Lady dogs all over Texas would go into mourning. County employees would lower the flag at the Twitchell courthouse, and Deputy Kile would remove his hat and dab moisture from his eyes.

Sally May would regret all the times she had screeched at me for wetting on her tires. Miss Beulah would weep. Miss Viola would wear a long black dress and a black veil for a whole month. Slim would sing a corny song at the funeral and Loper would probably put the ranch up for sale.

Pretty sad, huh? You bet.

I backed up as far as I could go, and the ape kept coming, his eyes flashing unholy light. I could hear his heavy breathing and wicked laughter rumbling in his throat.

I guess we've come to the end of the trail and there's not much story left to tell.

But wait, hold everything! Maybe there was one last avenue of escape, and you didn't even notice. Neither did I, because...well, because it would involve athletic ability that was unheard of in ordinary dogs, and we're talking about the skill of an acrobat and a tightrope walker, put together.

It came to me in a flash that there might be one way out of this deathtrap, but it had never been attempted by any dog in history. Are you ready to hear this?

THE GOOSENECK ON THE TRAILER! Yes, the same steel device upon which I had banged my head upon which. Remember that? What you never thought of was that it formed a bridge from the bed of the pickup up to the roof of the trailer!

On a normal day, I never would have considered climbing the gooseneck, and would have thought it an impassable fot...an impossible feat, that is, but this was definitely not a normal day, and by jiminy jack, I had every intention of doing it, impossible or not.

I sprang into the air, landed on the gooseneck, and struggled to keep my balance. The next part would be the real test, climbing a slick, narrow slab of steel that rose at a 45 degree angle and connected to the roof of the trailer.

Should I take it slow, like a guy walking a cable, or hit it hard and scramble like a striped monkey? I voted for the monkey version, hit Turbo Five and sprinted up the narrow, slick strip of narrowly slick steel. And you know what?

I MADE IT!

No kidding. Against impossible odds, I reached the summit of the roof of the trailer, and at that point I was...well, ready to crow, gloat, and mouth off, might as well admit it. I mean, restraint in victory has never been one of my strong points.

But then it struck me...hey, if one dog could do it, maybe two dogs could do it. Steel, for example. I decided to, uh, shut my beak, at least for a while, and wait to see what might happen next.

Looking down, I could see that the ape was bewildered, and so was his girlfriend, the little troublemaker. Her mouth puckered into a pout. "Now what are you going to do?"

He shrugged. "I can't climb that thing."

"Steel, if y'all are going to fight, hurry up! I have things to do."

"Okay, Scamp, I'll try."

He didn't look very confident about this, and he was right. It turned into a disaster. His body was built for wrecking things, not for gymnastics and ballet dancing. He leaped up on the gooseneck, lost a foot, scrambled, teetered, clawed the air, and fell like a bad load of hay.

WHOP!

Miss Scamper gave her head a slow shake. "Well, that was cute."

He picked himself off the ground. "I told you."

"If that's the best you can do, I'm leaving." She stuck her snooty little nose into the air and swept away.

Steel limped a few steps and spit some dirt out of his mouth, then his glare burned a path toward me. "You're a smarty-pants little jerk."

"Thanks."

"You made me look bad in front of my girlfriend."

"Me? What did I do?"

His crazy eyes moved from side to side. "I don't know, but you're really, really, really going to get it now."

"How's that going to work? I'm up here and you can't reach me."

"You know what I'm going to do?"

"No. I can hardly wait to hear."

He puffed himself up. “I’m going to…you see that trailer?”

“Yes, I’m standing on it.”

“Well, enjoy it while you can, smart guy, ‘cause in thirty minutes, it ain’t going to be there.”

“No kidding. You’re going to…what, eat it?”

“Yeah, and tear it to smithereens. You ever see a pit bull in action?”

“Never have.”

“This trailer is toast, and you’re even toaster!”

He stomped over to the trailer tires, clamped his jaws on one of them, and gave it a ferocious shake. Even up on the roof, I could feel the jolt. You know, I didn’t think he could actually destroy a stock trailer, but I wasn’t sure he couldn’t either. I mean, the guy was huge and more than slightly crazy.

A little voice inside my head urged me to keep my mouth shut, so I sat down and watched. It was scary. Clearly, the guy wasn’t kidding about wanting to destroy the trailer, but after thirty minutes of growling, biting, and stirring up dust, he was still working on that same tire.

Miss Scamper showed up again and marched over to him. “Now what are you doing?” He didn’t answer or even look at her. She moved closer to the tire and squinted at it. “Steel, ah,

your name's on this tire."

He stopped chewing. "No kidding?"

"Dummy, that's a *steel*-belted radial!" She looked up at me. "He thinks he can chew up a steel-belted radial."

"I know, I've been watching for half an hour. Is he like this all the time?"

"He, ah, has trouble with little stuff." She sighed and glanced around, then fluffed at her ears, fluttered her eyelashes, and smiled up at me. "Listen, you big old hairy thang, why don't you come down and see me some time?"

You probably think that my brain shorted out, my heart went pitty-pat, and I dived off the trailer. In other words, you think I was dumb enough to fall for her line again. Ha, no way! No sir, I had become a wiser dog, an older dog...

Okay, I thought about it, but just then I heard whistles and shouts and the sounds of cattle. Off to the east, the crew was coming in with the herd.

Miss Scamper heard it too and turned to the Tire King. "They're coming in with cows."

He was looking crazy again. "You called him a big old hairy thang."

She rolled her eyes. "Steel, ah, you need to scram. You know how Baxter is about dogs and cattle."

He shook his head. "Uh uh, too late, got to finish this, he's toast!"

"Oh my word. Well, you go right on, mister, I'm leaving."

She switched away and Steel went back to work, trying to destroy the stock trailer. I was left up on the roof, wondering if he would get it done.

Exposed On The Roof

Okay, where were we? Oh yes, it was a cold, gray, windy day in the fall, and I was watching as the roundup crew brought in a hundred head of cows and calves. This was weaning time, you might recall, down at Baxter's place, and I had given my cowboys permission to help with the gathering. We called it "neighboring," and... we've already discussed that.

You might also recall that nobody had invited me to the roundup, but I had volunteered my services anyway. See, I knew they would need my help in penning the herd and sorting off the cows. We call it Our Ground Game and it's a crucial part of the overall roundup strategy.

Horses and cowboys are important, don't get

me wrong, but the star player in any fall roundup is the DOG, and we're talking about a top-of-the-line, blue-ribbon cowdog, not some ordinary mutt that gets in the way and barks his head off. Ordinary mutts are an embarrassment to the profession, don't you know. They stand in the gates and cause stampedes, and they give the rest of us a black nose.

A black eye, I guess it should be. They give the rest of us a black eye and a bad reputation. They don't understand the fundamentals of the business and that's why some ranchers...a lot of them, actually, don't want dogs near the corrals on a roundup day.

I had spent most of my life trying to overcome this bad publicity, and correcting the false impression that ranch dogs are...well, dumb and worthless, and let me tell you, it had been a struggle. Overcoming the truth isn't as easy as you might suppose.

Wait, that doesn't sound right. Overcoming *false impressions* isn't as easy as you might suppose. There we go.

So, yes, I had volunteered for this mission to supervise the Ground Game and to more or less run the whole show, but then this crazy deal came up with Miss Scamper and her brain-dead boyfriend, the pit bull, who wanted to eat me but had decided to destroy the stock trailer first.

Hencely, until the cowboys came to my rescue and got Steel on a stout chain, I was out of the Ground Game. I was pretty sure they would be anxious to get me back on the field. I mean, the entire roundup strategy was at risk.

But then another thought popped up. I was standing on the roof of a sixteen-foot gooseneck stock trailer, a very peculiar place for a professional stock dog to be on a roundup day. And how would that look to a bunch of cowboy-jokers?

I knew exactly how it would look: ridiculous!

Oh brother, I had to hide! My eyes swept across the...if you've ever seen the roof of a stock trailer, you know that it's a five-by-sixteen foot slab of sheet metal, and it has no hiding places. None. Zero.

Okay, maybe if I scrunched down and lay perfectly flat and switched on Stealth, I would...I don't know, become invisible. Remember our discussion about naked eyes? Maybe...maybe their eyes would be so naked, they wouldn't notice me.

I had to give it a shot. I switched on Stealth, lay flat, and covered my eyes with my paws. Drover did that when he wanted to flee from

Reality, and maybe it would work for me.

I heard the moaning of the wind and the sounds of cattle: hooves on the ground, cows mooing for their calves and calves bawling for their mommas. A horse nickered and another answered back. A metal gate closed and a chain clinked...clanked...clunked...someone secured the gate with a chain, is the point.

They had penned the cattle and shut the gate.

So far, not a mocking word from the cowboys. Good. They hadn't seen me. I began to feel better about this. Once again, Stealth had worked and made me invisible to naked eyes and enemy radar. Whew! At last, I dared to uncover my eyes and look around.

Huh?

Down below, I saw three cowboys ahorseback: Baxter, Slim, and Loper. Their gazes prowled around, going from Steel up to me and back down to Steel. They shook their heads. Slim's chin dropped to his chest, and Loper rolled his eyes up to the sky.

SLIM: "What in the cat hair is going on here?"

BAXTER: "Well, my dog is trying to eat a tire, and there's another dog on top of your trailer. Anybody know that dog?"

SLIM: "Not me."

LOPER: "Never saw him before."

[Moment of silence]

SLIM: "Bax, I can't lie. That's Loper's dog."

LOPER: "He's your dog! He stayed at your house last night, and he acts just like you too."

BAXTER: "What do you reckon he's doing up there?"

LOPER: "Well, we can start with the fact that he's dumber than a pile of gravel."

SLIM: "Bax, I'll admit that we know the dog, but we didn't bring him, and I have no idea what he's doing up there."

BAXTER: "And I have no idea why Steel is

trying to eat a tire."

SLIM: "Makes you proud, don't it?"

They laughed. I didn't. This was one of the most embarrassing...how had this happened to me? After all my years of service...never mind. There wasn't one thing I could do about it.

Baxter got off his horse, gave Steel a scolding, and tied him to a post with a piece of rope, then the three of them rode into the corrals and started sorting off cows and calves—without my help. I mean, they just left me up there on the roof. Not only did I have to watch from the sidelines, but I had to breathe all the dust from the cattle work.

It took them an hour to do the sorting, then they ran the calves into the weaning pen, put out bales of prairie hay in three hay feeders, and poured out sacks of creep feed into some steel bunks.

I had to watch that too. It was one of the saddest days of my whole career.

At last they finished the job and my guys loaded their horses in the trailer. Oh, and did I mention that Snips saw me up there and ran his big fat mouth? He did. He snorted a horse laugh and said, "Good place to park a dog!"

Moron. Idiot.

Loper and Slim took off their chaps and

pitched them into the back of the pickup, and Slim pointed toward...well, up to me, I suppose. "There's only one way he could have gotten there. He had to climb up the gooseneck."

"Is he smart enough to climb down the same way?"

"I wouldn't bet on it." Slim whistled and slapped his thigh. "Come on, pooch, we're ready to go to the house. Climb down."

Climb down that steep, slick piece of steel? I went to Looks of Deep Regret and Slow Wags on the tail section, transmitting a sad message. "Guys, believe me, I'd love to help you out, but there's no way that will work. Sorry."

Slim scowled up at me. "Hank, come on."

Could you speak louder? We seem to have a bad connection.

"Hank!" Slim turned to Loper. "Now what?"

"Start climbing."

"Don't I have a vote? This is still America."

Loper smirked. "Yes, but out here, the boss counts the ballots. Go get 'im, cowboy."

Slim grumbled, hitched up his jeans, shot me a poisoned glare, climbed into the bed of the pickup, and started scooting his way up the gooseneck.

I was *so sorry* this had happened, but they

just didn't understand, and there was no way I could explain it through wags and nonverbal so-forths. They would just have to be mad.

Slim finally made it to the roof. "Come here, you meathead."

Oh brother. If you want a dog to come, do you call him *meathead*? Whatever happened to manners and charm and kindness?

"Hank!"

Oh all right, but don't forget the Ancient Proverb: "You can catch more flies with a fly-swatter, but a pencil must be lead."

Was that the Ancient Proverb? Maybe not, skip it.

The point is that Slim had no more manners than a goat, and it would have served him right if I had marched off in the opposite direction, but...well, there really wasn't anywhere to go, so...okay, I went to him.

He grabbed me by a front leg and dragged me into a boa constrictor embrace, and my claws made an awful screeching sound on the sheet metal roof. He called down to Loper. "Can you catch him?"

"I guess we'll find out."

Catch me? He was going to...forget that, Charlie! No way were those clowns going to...

He pitched me out into empty space and I began, well, dog-paddling, I guess you would say, moving my front paws in hopes of...I don't know what, but it didn't work. I plunged toward the ground and, much to my surprise, Loper caught me in his arms.

Hey, I was safe! I gave him a juicy lick on the face. I knew we could do it! Nice work!

So there you are, an example of how well things can turn out when we work together as a team. It all begins with a sound plan of action, and then you add the most important ingredient: *trust*. That trust is so important. Show me a ranch without trust and I'll show you a ranch where nobody trusts anybody.

So, yes, my plan worked to perfection. Slim had a little trouble getting down off the roof and seemed a bit crabby, but that was a small price to pay for a successful mission. I was proud of my guys.

Loper tossed me into the back of the pickup. Slim curled his lip and called me "Bozo," and we started back to the ranch. As we were pulling away from the corrals, we drove past Steel, who was still tied to a post. When he saw me, he leaped to his feet, started barking his head off, and lunged against the rope.

Oh gosh. He flipped over backwards and really busted himself on the ground. Hee hee. I couldn't resist yelling, "Hey Steel, show that trick to your girlfriend!"

He staggered to his feet and roared, "Next time I see you, jerk, you won't be laughing, oh yeah!"

Maybe I shouldn't have stuck out my tongue, but who could resist? I mean, he was tied up and I was driving away, and he deserved it. Furthermore and most important, I knew I would never see the big ape again.

So I stuck out my tongue! Hee hee.

The Dungeon Confession

We made it back to Slim's place around noon, and the moment the pickup came to a stop, I dived out of the back. Slim unloaded his mouthy crow-bait of a horse and led him down to the saddle shed. Loper drove back to headquarters.

I noticed that Snips was chuckling and shaking his head. Does anybody care what a horse thinks? No. Slim pulled off the saddle and gave him oats and three blocks of nice green alfalfa. I would have given him sawdust.

Moron.

Slim closed up the saddle shed and all at once we were alone. I noticed that he was looking down at me. "I should have flushed you down the pot when I had the chance."

Was that any way to talk to a friend?

"You're a disobedient whelp of a dog."

I was just trying to help!

He leaned down so that our noses were almost touching. "For future reference, dog, any time we go to help the neighbors, you ain't invited. Is there any part of that you don't understand?"

I mistered the mustard...let's try that again. I must have misunderstood.

He looked at me for a long time, then a teenie smile twitched at one corner of his mouth. "Was that dog pretty tough?"

Who? What dog?

"He looked kind of scary."

Oh, him? He was a creampuff with a big mouth.

"That's what I figured. Roosting on top of the trailer was probably the smartest thing you've done all year."

Well, thanks...I guess.

"But you're still a disobedient whelp of a dog, and I have to stay mad at you for an hour, else you'll do it again next time."

I hung my head. I would never do it again, honest. Never.

"Go sit on the porch."

He walked away.

Pretty sad, huh? You bet, but let me share a

secret. In small but tiny ways, I had brought this punishment on myself, and Slim had a particle of truth on his side. See, I had a weakness for doing Slightly Naughty Things. It had been a problem most of my life and, yes, I needed to work on it.

And I *would* work on it. For the next hour, while Slim was patching on the corral fence, I would have a stern talk with myself and get a handle on my problem, before it got out of hand.

I hiked up to the house, flopped down on the porch, and launched into this bold venture. You know what I did? You'll be amazed. I visited myself in a dark dungeon cell, and Me and Myself did a song about my problem. Would you like to hear it? I guess it wouldn't hurt. Check this out.

Dungeon Confession

MYSELF

Hank, you were a naughty dog.
Now your cowboy pals are mad.
Surely you must feel some guilt.
Tell me now how bad it is.

ME

Yes, I knew that I messed up.
"Disobedient," he said.
Boy, the load was piling up.
Broke my heart in fifty pieces.

MYSELF

Can you guess the weight of guilt?
More like feathers or in tons?

ME

Tons of guilt there at the first,
Feathers now, and maybe ten.

MYSELF

True confession brings relief.
Turns our pockets wrong-side-out.

ME

Yes, I think it's really helped
Lighten the awful load of guilt.

MYSELF

But, my son, the question now
Is if you had another chance,
Would you sneak into the truck
And to a roundup go again?

ME

That's the question, isn't it?
Funny that you should have asked.
I was wondering myself
And I think I probably would.
Yes.

So there you are. The next time you see a dog sitting on the porch and wearing a sad expression, don't assume that he's just loafing or thinking "duh." He might be having a deep conversation with himself about his Naughty Dogness. It's something every dog should do at least once a month.

Well! I had done my duty and now it was time to get back to my life. I sprang to my feet, gave myself a good shake, and noticed...Drover. He was sitting on the south edge of the porch, staring off into space.

I went over to him. "Hello? Anybody home?"

His eyes drifted down and he gave me his usual silly grin.

"Oh, hi. Did you just wake up?"

"Drover, I was up before daylight and just got back from supervising a roundup."

"I'll be derned."

"Have you been sitting here all morning?"

"No, I was sitting over there for a while, then moved over here. I got bored."

"You got bored. You know, one of these days, you should try *doing* something. Had you thought of that?"

He yawned. "Yeah, I thought about it once, but it seemed like a lot of trouble."

"Oh brother."

He yawned again. "How was the roundup?"

"It was the most exciting event you've missed in months. I'll tell you about it, if you'll stop yawning."

"Drat. Just one more?"

"Okay, one more and that's it."

He took a big one, and even threw an arch in his back and stretched his legs. That was probably the most exercise he'd gotten in months. He grinned. "Okay, I'm ready."

"Sit down and try to pay attention."

He sat down and I launched into a full disclosure of the morning's events. When I sensed that his attention was wandering (that happens a lot with Drover), I goosed the story a bit, you know, to keep it interesting.

He listened with fried-egg eyes, and even gasped several times. "You gathered and sorted the cattle all by yourself?"

"That's correct, yes. For the most part."

"And you did tricks for Miss Scamper?"

"You bet. Let me tell you, son, that double back-flip off the roof of the barn really sealed the deal. Of course her boyfriend threw a jealous fit."

"She had a boyfriend?"

"I didn't mention that? Oh yes, big dude." I leaned toward him. "He was a professional fighting *pit bull.*"

The runt gasped so hard, he sucked in a gnat and went into a coughing fit. "A pit bull! Oh my gosh, I'm scared of those guys. What happened?"

"Well, I didn't want to make a scene, but he kept running his big yap, so I thrashed him on the spot."

His eyes grew even bigger. "No fooling? You whipped a pit bull?"

"Whipped him so bad, he climbed up on the roof of the stock trailer and sang 'Jingle Bells'." Drover's eyes crossed, so I knew he'd enjoyed the story. "Now, if you'll excuse me, I'm going to take a nap. It was a great morning, but I'm a little tired. Hold my calls."

I went to the mat in front of the door, scratched around on it, did the Three Turns Procedure, and flopped down. Within seconds, I was snort murf honk snicklefritz mousing broccoli dictionaries zzzzzzzzzzzzzzzzzzzzzzz.

Perhaps I dozed. Yes, of course I dozed. That's the whole idea behind taking a nap, right? But then I heard a voice.

"Oh my gosh! Hank, you'd better wake up!"

Wake up from what? And who was Hank? I sat up and opened my eyes. There, in front of my opened eyes, stood...something. A dog? Yes,

some dog-looking life form, and his teeth were clacking.

"Who are you and what's wrong with your teeth?"

"Oh my gosh, Hank, remember that pit bull you beat up? I think HE'S COMING THIS WAY!"

Huh?

Uh Oh, Big Trouble

I sprang to my feet and shook the vapors out of my ears...out of my eyes...out of my head...I shook the vapors out of something, it was very confusing, and stared at a dog in front of me.

"Wait a second, are you Drover?"

"Yeah, hi."

"Hi. Did you say something about spit balls?"

"No, I said *pit bull* and he's heading this way."

"Why wasn't I informed? How can I command this ship when we're being bombarded with spit balls?" I blinked my eyes. "Did you say pit bull?"

His teeth were clacking. "Yeah, look."

"Stop clacking your teeth." I dashed to the control room and did a sweep with field glasses. "Good grief, that's a pit bull!"

"That's what I said. What are we going to do?"

Bad memories came rushing back and my mouth was suddenly very dry. "Okay, men, listen up. We're going to send out an emissary with a white flag."

"Not me."

"And we're looking for a volunteer. Drover, do you have any white flags?"

"Just my tail."

"Perfect."

"But it's a stub. I don't think it would work."

"It'll work fine."

"Everybody makes fun of it."

"That doesn't matter. It's the thought that counts."

"Yeah, and here's a thought. I'm out of here!"

I heard a swish of air, and saw white hairs and flakes of dandruff floating through a sunbeam. "Drover?" He was gone. "Drover, come back here, and that is a direct order! Drover? You will be court-martialed for this!"

I took another glimpse with field glasses, hoping…gulp, it was a pit bull, all right. Steel.

Well, my emissary had noodled out on me and we had hit the bottom of the options barrel. I'd had a pretty good life, a few ups and downs and a few good laughs, but somewhere on Life's Journey,

I should have learned to keep my big mouth shut around gorillas.

Surely someone in my past had warned me not to mouth off to pit bulls. And not to flirt with their girlfriends.

Sigh. Well, when Slim returned, he would find strips of dog jerky hanging from the tree limbs, and a spot of grease in front of the house.

With the sounds of Steel's footsteps in my ears, I slipped into my breast plate, buckled on my sword, and placed the red-plumed helmet on my head. In those precious last moments, I thought of...well, Mom, of course. She tried so hard.

I took a big gulp of air and rode out to battle. From the porch, the enemy had looked big. As we moved closer to each other, he looked enormous, something huge and hideous.

Ten feet away from him, I stopped. He stopped. Our eyes locked. I tried to hide the quiver in my voice. "Steel, you're trespassing on my ranch, and I guess you don't have a permission slip."

"That's right."

"Sometimes in these situations, the trespasser just turns around and goes back home. Is that something you'd consider doing?"

"Nah."

"So that leaves...well, a fight to the death, I guess."

There was a throbbing moment of silence. I held my breath, then he said, "You've got it wrong. I came to say...I'm sorry."

My eyes bugged out. "What!" Only then did I notice that his face seemed...well, sad.

He continued. "You were right. Me and you don't have anything to fight about. Why should we bust our heads over Scamper? She's always been, well...a scamp."

"You really mean that?"

"Oh yeah, and...you know, dude, I ain't got many friends, nobody to talk to. I mean, you say 'pit bull' and everybody faints. It's a reputation deal and we can't shake it." His eyes grew misty. "Reckon we could talk, just you and me, dog to dog?"

I was stunned. "Well, I...sure, you bet. Let's go to my office and get comfortable."

Can you believe this? Wow.

We walked back to the porch, side by side like two old warriors who had put away the hatchets and swords, brass knuckles and butcher knives. We found a sunny spot on the porch and sat down.

I started things off. “Steel, it took a lot of courage for you to do this.”

“Yeah, maybe, but here’s the thing. A guy gets tired of being a meathead. He’s got to try something different, know what I mean?”

“Exactly right, which reminds me of something my dear mother told me. She looked into my eyes and said, ‘Hank, son, Life is a choice between Smart and Stupid. Once in a while, choose Smart.’”

Steel burst out laughing. “No kidding? Hey, you ain’t going to believe this, but that’s what my ma said to me!”

We laughed and shared this tender moment, then I moved the conversation into heavier stuff. “Steel, how did you get mixed up with Scamper?”

He looked off into the distance. “I wonder. I guess I thought she was cute.”

“I understand. That was my first impression too.”

“The first day we met, she looked at me and said, ‘Hello there, you big old hairy thang!’”

I laughed. “She said that? Steel, she said exactly the same thing to me.”

“Nah! Really?”

“Honest. It’s the oldest line in the books.”

“Yeah, but did you fall for it?”

"At first maybe, but then I saw it for what it was, lame and insincere."

He shook his head. "Well, I fell for it. I must be some kind of dummy."

I moved closer and placed a paw on his shoulder. It felt like cement. "Don't be too hard on yourself, old pardner. She's just a little troublemaker."

"She really is. You tried to tell me and I didn't listen, and we almost got into a big fight." He blinked his eyes and a tear rolled down his cheek. "Can I tell you one more thing? Are we good enough friends?"

"Oh sure, yes. Let's get it out, all of it. This is the time for Truth."

He glanced around and lowered his voice. "I'm a pit bull, right? But I ain't all that good at fighting."

"No kidding! Boy, you sure fooled me."

"I know. I look mean, but fighting kind of goes against my nature, you see what I'm saying?"

"I had no idea, Steel. And now I'll confide in you. I'm not crazy about fighting either."

He laughed and shook his head. "That's funny. There we were, ready to tear each other to pieces...over her!"

I gave his shoulder another pat. "Steel, I'm so

glad we've had this chance to share. I think we've made real progress. The bottom line is... she's no good."

"You nailed it, bud. She's a fake and a fraud and a little troublemaker."

"And now we're rid of her, both of us, forever!"

It was a very touching scene, two old enemies making peace and coming to a new, life-changing understanding. It was one of those golden moments that, well, shine in your memory like a shining, golden moment.

But just then, we heard something, perhaps the sound of a vehicle. Steel raised one ear and cut his eyes from side to side. "That's Baxter. He's looking for me."

"Are you sure?"

He listened again. "Yeah, fan belt's loose, it squeals. I'd know it anywhere."

"Well, are you ready to go back home? Have we worked through your issues?"

He nodded and smiled. "Yeah, and I really appreciate your help, man."

"Glad to do it."

Sure enough, it was Baxter's pickup, an old faded-red Ford half-ton. He stopped in front of the saddle shed and blew the horn. Slim came out. "Hey, Bax, what's up?"

"You seen my dog?"

"Nope, sure haven't." He looked toward the porch and saw us. "Yes, I have. Lookie yonder, it's Laurel and Hardy of the dog world."

Baxter laughed. I didn't get the joke, but that was nothing new. Those guys are always goofing off about something and a dog is lucky to understand half of what they say.

They started a conversation about the cattle market and grass conditions, but then...

You won't believe this part. Another dog had been lying down in the back of the pickup, see, and all at once she stood up and...it was a lady dog, kind of pretty in a cheap sort of way, and she smiled at us and wiggled her eyebrows, both of them at once, and said, "Well, ah, hello there, boys! What's, ah, going on around here?"

I heard air rushing into Steel's chest. "It's her! She'll try to stir up trouble again."

My mind was racing. "We can't allow it, Steel, and I've got a plan. Let's turn our backs and ignore her!"

He grinned. "Oh yeah, that'll drive her nuts."

"Yes, because she always wants to be the center of attention, right?"

"You nailed it, bud."

And right there, in front of everybody, we

turned our backs on the little agitator and concentrated all our powers on not paying her the least bit of attention.

Was this awesome or what! My pal and I could hardly hold back our laughter. But then… wait, what was that? A voice? Yes, a voice, and it said, "Oh my gosh, Miss Scamper, I think I'm in love!"

Hold onto your chair and get ready for a big shock.

A Stunning Conclusion, No Kidding

Are you ready for the big shock? That was DROVER'S VOICE!

Steel was surprised. So was I. We turned and looked. Both our mouths dropped open and we stared into each other's eyes. Then he said, "Who is that guy?"

"Steel, I hate to admit this, but he's on my staff, a little slacker named Drover."

"He works for you?"

"More or less, but don't tell anyone. I'm going to fire him just as soon as everyone leaves."

"He don't act very smart."

"Believe me, he's not. He's an embarrassment to the entire Security Division. Every time a lady dog shows up, he loses his mind."

"Poor little guy. I used to be that way, but now I don't care about her. Do you?"

"Not at all, Steel. We've been through the childish stuff and we're in this thing together."

He gave me a smile and draped his big paw on my shoulder, and we watched with a kind of mature sadness as the runt made a fool of himself.

He was acting deranged. He bent his body into the shape of a horseshoe, wiggled his stub tail, rolled on the ground, and dragged himself around on his belly. It was shocking, embarrassing, pure silliness. Miss Scamper glanced over at us (we totally ignored her) and looked down at Little Romeo.

She fluttered her eyelashes and fluffed at her ears. "Well, hello there, you little old hairy thang! Why don't, ah, you hop your bad self into the, ah, pickup?"

Huh?

Steel and I exchanged a long glance, and I said, "Don't worry, he'll never make it into the pickup."

And he whispered back, "Well, I don't care anyway."

"Right. Neither do I."

We continued to watch the sad spectacle.

Drover leaped to his feet and started hopping around like...I don't know, like some kind of kangaroo. Then he sprang upward, hooked his front paws on the tailgate, clawed and scratched and scrambled, and...

I couldn't believe it. He actually tumbled into the back of the pickup! "I made it, Miss Scamper, and what do you think now?"

She drew herself up and batted her lashes. "Well, ah, I think I'm almost impressed!"

A growl leaped out of Steel's throat, and he lost whatever pleasant expression he'd had before. "Hey, what's the deal here?"

"Take it easy, old buddy, let me handle this. You sit tight. Are you okay? Talk to me."

"I'm okay. You handle it."

Whew! That was a bad look in his eyes, I mean like the flash that comes off a welding rod. In other words, Steel might have worked through his issues, but this was a can of worms we didn't want to put into Pandowdy's Box.

I left him sitting on the porch and rushed over to the pickup. There, I saw Drover in his pathetic state—hopping up and down, his tongue hanging out and eyes rolling around inside his head.

It was time to put a stop to this. "Drover, halt, cease!"

The edge in my voice seemed to jerk him back to the real world. "Oh, hi. Do you see who's here? Oh my gosh!"

"Drover, listen carefully. I am giving you a direct order: go to your room immediately!"

"Yeah, but…"

"Now! Or you will stand with your nose in the corner for three weeks."

His head sank. "Oh drat."

"Go!"

He slithered over the tailgate, landed on the ground, and crept off to the porch, sniffling and whining on every step.

I turned a cold gaze up to the troublemaker. "Miss Scamper, you ought to be ashamed of yourself. He's just a little dunce."

"He, ah, seemed so sincere."

"He's sincerely daffy."

She lifted an eyebrow. "Oh really? How about you?"

"Huh? Me? Ha, ha. I'm not daffy at all, ma'am. In fact, I'm Head of the entire Security Division."

"That's, ah, what I've heard."

"And as you know, I'm something of a musician. How about another song?"

She coughed. "Oh, let's don't."

"Then...maybe a poem? How about a poem?" I wiggled my left eyebrow. That's the one that really grabs the ladies, the left one.

It worked! She smiled. "Sure. Let's see what you've got."

Wow, you talk about eyes bugging out and a heart beating like a truckload of beating hearts! How many dogs get a chance like this? Somehow I had to compose a knockout poem right there, on the spot, without any kind of preparation.

Could I do it? I took a wide stance and looked into her adoring gaze.

Ode To A Fair Lady

Miss Scamper, at one time I thought you
were trouble.
You turned all the local dogs' brains into
bubbles.
It even occurred to me that your delight
Was making us jealous and stirring up
fights.

But time and reflection hath altered my mind.
I had no idea that your taste was refined.
Your interest in literature blows me away,
And here's an idea: Let's do poetry all day!

I gazed up at her. "What did you think of that one, huh?"

"Well, I hardly know what to say. You, ah, wrote that yourself?"

"Oh yes ma'am, on the spot and just for you."

"Oooo! I wonder if, ah, you could jump your big bad self up here and do another one."

"Heh. I think we can arrange that." I went into Deep Crouch and sprang like a deer, cleared the tailgate and landed in the back of the pickup beside her.

She uttered a little gasp. "My, my, you're so athletic!"

"Yeah, well, wait until you hear this next poem. You'll think athletic!"

I lifted my head to an angle that was just right for delivering a knockout literary effort, took a big gulp of...

A hacksaw voice cut through the silence. "Hey! What are you doing up there?"

What...who...? I turned my head and saw... oops. Maybe you had forgotten about Steel. Maybe I had too, but here he came. Tromp, tromp, tromp. And, well, that's about the end of the story, because nothing happened.

Almost nothing happened, and if anything happened, you don't need to know about it. Don't forget: *the little children.*

So that's the end of the story. It's time to brush our teeth and go to bed. This case is closed. Goodbye.

[LONG SILENCE]

Okay, the case isn't as closed as you thought. There's more. You're still here, and I guess we might as well come clean on this.

Remember that deep and meaningful conversation I had with Steel on the porch? He said something about not being a very good fighter, in spite of being a pit bull. Remember that?

Well, let me tell you something. He was either being very modest or lying through his bulldog teeth. The guy was a DRAGON. He wrecked me so fast, I didn't even land a punch.

He came pouring over the tailgate like an invasion force of jealous Marines. I was, well, surprised. "Steel, could we talk about this?"

For the record, he said nothing. His eyes were blazing and his answer seemed to be that no, he didn't want to talk.

Once in the bed of the pickup, he took a bite on the loose skin on the back of my neck, flung me around like a bullwhip, and sent me sailing high in the air, far away from his pouty little girlfriend.

As I flew past Slim Chance, I heard him say, "Good honk, is that a UFO or my dog?"

Always making jokes. Well, it was no joke to me. I hit the ground like a hunk of space debris, skidded several yards, and got a mouthful of fresh dirt. By the time I staggered to my feet, Baxter was driving away and I saw...

Steel stood proud in the back of the pickup like some kind of statue, and his empty-headed trouble-making girlfriend was just gaga over him. And I heard her say, "Oooo! I hope that wasn't over me!"

Yeah, right. Oh well, they deserved each other, and I was glad to be rid of them. Let's be perfectly clear: I DIDN'T CARE.

I limped toward the porch, past Slim, the local comedian. He was biting back a grin and couldn't resist making a comment. He said, and this is a direct quote, he said, "Pooch, if you keep flying around like that, we may need to get you a pilot's license."

Pilot's license. Was that funny? Does anyone in the world see humor in that? No. It was lame, stale, disrespectful, and...phooey.

I limped back to the porch and sat down. Drover sat nearby and said, "How'd it go?" I answered him with a stony silence. "Hank, she's no good."

I roasted him with a glare. "If she's so no-good, how come you turned into a gasping, squeaking, brainless little ninny?"

"Well, you did too. I saw it myself."

"Okay, that's it! Ten Chicken Marks and you will stand with your nose in the corner for a month—now! March!"

He whined and cried, but I had no sympathy. He stuck his nose in the southwest corner of the porch and I sat down beside him, to make sure he didn't cheat. If I hadn't stood guard, he would have cheated, and do you know why? Because he had spent so many idle hours hanging out with the local cat.

Five minutes into his prison term, Drover said, "If she's the one who's no good, how come I'm the one who has to stand in the corner?"

"Because, Drover, Life is very complicated. Think about that and stop yapping."

And that's about the end of the story. It wasn't the happiest ending we've ever come up with, but the impointant poink is that I had become a wiser dog, a stronger dog, more mature in the ways of the world.

Miss Scamper was no good and this case is closed.

Have you read all of Hank's adventures?

1 *The Original Adventures of Hank the Cowdog*
2 *The Further Adventures of Hank the Cowdog*
3 *It's a Dog's Life*
4 *Murder in the Middle Pasture*
5 *Faded Love*
6 *Let Sleeping Dogs Lie*
7 *The Curse of the Incredible Priceless Corncob*
8 *The Case of the One-Eyed Killer Stud Horse*
9 *The Case of the Halloween Ghost*
10 *Every Dog Has His Day*
11 *Lost in the Dark Unchanted Forest*
12 *The Case of the Fiddle-Playing Fox*
13 *The Wounded Buzzard on Christmas Eve*
14 *Hank the Cowdog and Monkey Business*
15 *The Case of the Missing Cat*
16 *Lost in the Blinded Blizzard*
17 *The Case of the Car-Barkaholic Dog*

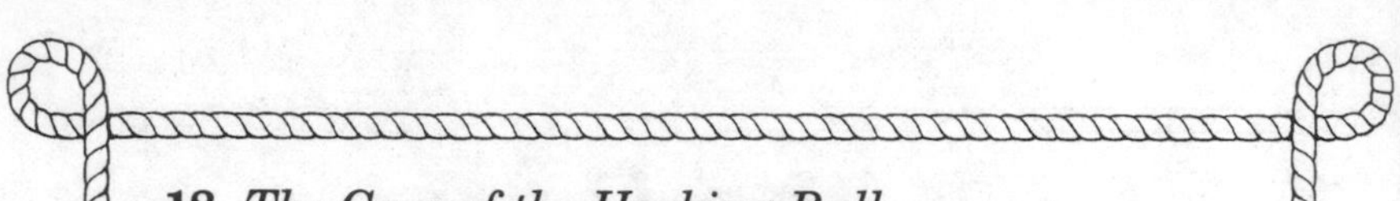

18 *The Case of the Hooking Bull*
19 *The Case of the Midnight Rustler*
20 *The Phantom in the Mirror*
21 *The Case of the Vampire Cat*
22 *The Case of the Double Bumblebee Sting*
23 *Moonlight Madness*
24 *The Case of the Black-Hooded Hangmans*
25 *The Case of the Swirling Killer Tornado*
26 *The Case of the Kidnapped Collie*
27 *The Case of the Night-Stalking Bone Monster*
28 *The Mopwater Files*
29 *The Case of the Vampire Vacuum Sweeper*
30 *The Case of the Haystack Kitties*
31 *The Case of the Vanishing Fishhook*
32 *The Garbage Monster from Outer Space*
33 *The Case of the Measled Cowboy*
34 *Slim's Good-bye*
35 *The Case of the Saddle House Robbery*
36 *The Case of the Raging Rottweiler*
37 *The Case of the Deadly Ha-Ha Game*
38 *The Fling*
39 *The Secret Laundry Monster Files*
40 *The Case of the Missing Bird Dog*
41 *The Case of the Shipwrecked Tree*
42 *The Case of the Burrowing Robot*
43 *The Case of the Twisted Kitty*
44 *The Dungeon of Doom*
45 *The Case of the Falling Sky*
46 *The Case of the Tricky Trap*
47 *The Case of the Tender Cheeping Chickies*
48 *The Case of the Monkey Burglar*

49 *The Case of the Booby-Trapped Pickup*
50 *The Case of the Most Ancient Bone*
51 *The Case of the Blazing Sky*
52 *The Quest for the Great White Quail*
53 *Drover's Secret Life*
54 *The Case of the Dinosaur Birds*
55 *The Case of the Secret Weapon*
56 *The Case of the Coyote Invasion*
57 *The Disappearance of Drover*
58 *The Case of the Mysterious Voice*
59 *The Case of the Perfect Dog*
60 *The Big Question*
61 *The Case of the Prowling Bear*
62 *The Ghost of Rabbits Past*
63 *The Return of the Charlie Monsters*
64 *The Case of the Three Rings*
65 *The* Almost *Last Roundup*
66 *The Christmas Turkey Disaster*
67 *Wagons West*
68 *The Secret Pledge*
69 *The Case of the Wandering Goats*
70 *The Case of the Troublesome Lady*

Join Hank the Cowdog's Security Force

Are you a big Hank the Cowdog fan? Then you'll want to join Hank's Security Force! Here is some of the neat stuff you will receive:

Welcome Package

- A Hank paperback
- An Original (19"x25") Hank Poster
- A Hank bookmark

Eight digital issues of *The Hank Times* with

- Lots of great games and puzzles
- Stories about Hank and his friends
- Special previews of future books
- Fun contests

More Security Force Benefits

- Special discounts on Hank books, audios, and more
- Special Members-Only section on website

Total value of the Welcome Package and *The Hank Times* is $23.99. However, your two-year membership is **only $7.99** plus $5.00 for shipping and handling.

☐ Yes I want to join Hank's Security Force. Enclosed is $12.99 ($7.99 + $5.00 for shipping and handling) for my **two-year membership**. [Make check payable to Maverick Books.]

Which book would you like to receive in your Welcome Package? (#) any book except #50

BOY or GIRL
YOUR NAME (CIRCLE ONE)

MAILING ADDRESS

CITY STATE ZIP

TELEPHONE BIRTH DATE

E-MAIL (required for digital Hank Times)

Send check or money order for $12.99 to:

Hank's Security Force
Maverick Books
PO Box 549
Perryton, Texas 79070

DO NOT SEND CASH. NO CREDIT CARDS ACCEPTED.

Allow 2–3 weeks for delivery.

Offer is subject to change.

We all know Hank loves to eat... and now *you* can try some of his favorite recipes!

Have you visited Sally May's Kitchen yet?

http://www.hankthecowdog.com/recipes

***Here, you'll find recipes for*:**

Sally May's Apple Pie

Hank's Picante Sauce

Round-Up Green Beans

Little Alfred's and Baby Molly's Favorite Cookies

Cowboy Hamburgers with Gravy

Chicken-Ham Casserole

...and MORE!

Early Morning Round-Up Burritos Recipe

Ingredients:

- 8 Eggs
- 8-10 Strips of Bacon
- 1/2 Onion (chopped)
- 1/2 Bell Pepper (chopped)
- Salt & Pepper
- 8 Tortillas
- 1 c. Cheddar Cheese
- Pico de gallo

Instructions:

1. Fry bacon in a cast-iron skillet until crispy. Once the bacon is cool, crumble the strips into pieces and set aside in a bowl.
2. Pour most of the bacon grease out of the skillet, leaving just enough in the pan to use for sauteeing the onions and bell peppers together.
3. While the vegetables are cooking, whisk the eggs with a few tablespoons of water (or milk), and add salt and pepper to your taste.
4. When onions and peppers are soft, add in the eggs and cook until the eggs are no longer runny.
5. Add cooked pieces of bacon to the mixture.
6. Sprinkle cheese over the top, then fill tortillas with however much of the mixture each person wants!

The following activities are samples from *The Hank Times*, the official newspaper of Hank's Security Force. Please do not write on these pages unless this is your book. And, even then, why not just find a scrap of paper?

"Photogenic" Memory Quiz

We all know that Hank has a "photogenic" memory—being aware of your surroundings is an important quality for a Head of Ranch Security. Now *you* can test your powers of observation.

How good is your memory? Look at the illustration on page 15 and try to remember as many things about it as possible. Then turn back to this page and see how many questions you can answer.

1. How many drawers were there? 1, 2, or 3?
2. Was Slim wearing boots? Yes or No?
3. What time was it? 4:00, 5:00, 6:00, or 7:00?
4. Was the spider on the *left* or *right* side of the clock?
5. Was Slim looking *up* or *down*?
6. How many *dog's* eyes could you see? 2, 3, 4, or all 5?

"Word Maker"

Try making up to twenty words from the letters in the name below. Use as many letters as possible, however, don't just add an "s" to a word you've already listed in order to have it count as another. Try to make up entirely new words for each line!

Then, count the total number of letters used in all of the words you made, and see how well you did using the Security Force Rankings below!

MISS SCAMPER

____________________	____________________
____________________	____________________
____________________	____________________
____________________	____________________
____________________	____________________
____________________	____________________
____________________	____________________
____________________	____________________
____________________	____________________
____________________	____________________

59-61 You spend too much time with J.T. Cluck and the chickens.

62-64 You are showing some real Security Force potential.

65-68 You have earned a spot on our Ranch Security team.

69+ Wow! You rank up there as a top-of-the-line cowdog.

"Rhyme Time"

What if Baxter decides that he wants to leave his life of ranching and go in search of other jobs? What kinds of jobs could he find?

Make a rhyme using "BAX" that would relate to his new job possibilities.

Example: Baxter invents a game played with little, spikey metal objects..

Answer: Bax JACKS

1. Baxter becomes an accountant helping people file forms.
2. Baxter builds railroad roads.
3. Baxter makes bird hunting aids.
4. Baxter becomes a chiropractor.
5. Baxter invents new book-carrying device for school kids.
6. Baxter gets a job at a grocery store.
7. Baxter becomes a test-driver, finding things top speed.
8. Baxter starts a windshield repair shop.
9. Baxter start a roadside tire repair service.

Answers:

1. Bax TAX
2. Bax TRACKS
3. Bax QUACKS
4. Bax BACKS
5. Bax PACKS
6. Bax SACKS
7. Bax MAX
8. Bax CRACKS
9. Bax JACKS

search the website GO

BOOKS The Collection

FAN ZONE Fun & Games

AUTHOR Meet the Creator

STORE Books & More

Find Toys, Games, Books & More
at the Hank shop.

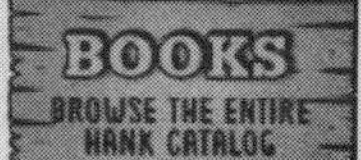

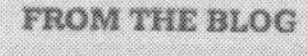

JAN 26 Hank is Cupid in Disguise...

JAN 18 The Valentine's Day Robbery! - a Snippet from the Story

DEC 04 Getting SIGNED Hank the Cowdog books for Christmas!

OCT 14 Education Association's lists of recommended books?

VISIT THE BLOG

Hank's Survey
We'd love to know what you think! GO

Hank's Music
Free ringtones, music and more!
MORE

Official Shop
Find books, audio, toys and more!
LET'S GO

TEACHER'S CORNER
Download fun activity guides, discussion questions and more.

SALLY MAY'S RECIPES
Discover delicious recipes from Sally May herself. GO

Join Hank's Security Force
Get the activity letter and other cool stuff.
JOIN

Visit Hank's Facebook page

Follow Hank on Twitter

Watch Hank on YouTube

Follow Hank on Pinterest

Send Hank an Email

Get the Latest
Keep up with Hank's news and promotions by signing up for our e-news.
Looking for The Hank Times fan club newsletter?
Enter your email address
SIGN UP

Hank in the News

Find out what the media is saying about Hank. GO

The Christmas Turkey Disaster
Now Available!
Hank is in real trouble this time. L...

BUY READ LISTEN

HANK

BOOKS
Browse Titles
Buy Books

FAN ZONE
Games
Hank & Friends

AUTHOR
John Erickson's Bio
Hank in the News

SHOP
The Books
Store

And, be sure to check out the Audiobooks!

If you've never heard a *Hank the Cowdog* audiobook, you're missing out on a lot of fun! Each Hank book has also been recorded as an unabridged audiobook for the whole family to enjoy!

Praise for the Hank Audiobooks:

"It's about time the Lone Star State stopped hogging Hank the Cowdog, the hilarious adventure series about a crime solving ranch dog. Ostensibly for children, the audio renditions by author John R. Erickson are sure to build a cult following among adults as well." — *Parade Magazine*

"Full of regional humor . . . vocals are suitably poignant and ridiculous. A wonderful yarn." — *Booklist*

"For the detectin' and protectin' exploits of the canine Mike Hammer, hang Hank's name right up there with those of other anthropomorphic greats...But there's no sentimentality in Hank: he's just plain more rip-roaring fun than the others. Hank's misadventures as head of ranch security on a spread somewhere in the Texas Panhandle are marvelous situation comedy." — *School Library Journal*

"Knee-slapping funny and gets kids reading."

— *Fort Worth Star Telegram*

Love Hank's Hilarious Songs?

Hank the Cowdog's "Greatest Hits" albums bring together the music from the unabridged audiobooks you know and love! These wonderful collections of hilarious (and sometimes touching) songs are unmatched. Where else can you learn about coyote philosophy, buzzard lore, why your dog is protecting an old corncob, how bugs compare to hot dog buns, and much more!

And, be sure to visit Hank's "Music Page" on the official website to listen to some of the songs and download FREE Hank the Cowdog ringtones!

"Audio-Only" Stories

Ever wondered what those "Audio-Only" Stories in Hank's Official Store are all about?

The Audio-Only Stories are Hank the Cowdog adventures that have never been released as books. They are about half the length of a typical Hank book, and there are currently seven of them. They have run as serial stories in newspapers for years and are now available as audiobooks!

Teacher's Corner

Know a teacher who uses Hank in their classroom? You'll want to be sure they know about Hank's "Teacher's Corner"! Just click on the link on the homepage, and you'll find free teacher's aids, such as a printable map of Hank's ranch, a reading log, coloring pages, blog posts specifically for teachers and librarians, and much more!

Photo Courtesy of Western Horseman Magazine

John R. Erickson, a former cowboy, has written numerous books for both children and adults and is best known for his acclaimed *Hank the Cowdog* series. The *Hank* series began as a self-publishing venture in Erickson's garage in 1982 and has endured to become one of the nation's most popular series for children and families.

Through the eyes of Hank the Cowdog, a smelly, smart-aleck Head of Ranch Security, Erickson gives readers a glimpse into daily life on a cattle ranch in the West Texas Panhandle. His stories have won a number of awards, including the Audie, Oppenheimer, Wrangler, and Lamplighter Awards, and have been translated into Spanish, Danish, Farsi, and Chinese. *USA Today* calls the *Hank the Cowdog* books "the best family entertainment in years." Erickson lives and works on his ranch in Perryton, Texas, with his family.

Shawn Tevis Photography

Gerald L. Holmes is a largely self-taught artist who grew up on a ranch in Oklahoma. For over thirty-five years, he has illustrated the *Hank the Cowdog* books and serial stories, as well as numerous other cartoons and textbooks, and his paintings have been featured in various galleries across the United States. He and his wife live in Perryton, Texas, where they raised their family, and where he continues to paint his wonderfully funny and accurate portrayals of modern American ranch life to this day.